The Disappearance
of Odile

GEORGES SIMENON

The Disappearance
of Odile

Translated from the French by Lyn Moir

A Helen and Kurt Wolff Book

Harcourt Brace Jovanovich, Inc., New York

Originally published in French under the title
La Disparition d'Odile

ISBN 0-15-125720-5
Library of Congress Catalog Card Number: 72-75422
Printed in the United States of America
BCDE

The Disappearance
of Odile

Chapter 1

Bob had got up at seven o'clock as usual. He had no need of an alarm clock. There were two of them in the family who organized their time like clockwork.

At that hour his father, who got up much earlier than he, had finished dressing and would be in the dining room, drinking the enormous cup of coffee that was all he had for breakfast, before taking his morning walk.

When Bob opened the curtains the sun burst suddenly into the room, and the luminous disk, which moved from place to place according to the seasons, quivered on the mirror.

It was the end of September, and since the beginning of the month not one drop of rain had fallen. The sky had not even been covered over, except for a few pale clouds that sailed slowly across the sky like boats on the sea.

He had shaved, then taken a quick shower. At half past seven he went downstairs. There was no one in

3

the dining room. His place was set, as was his sister's, but Odile did not get up until much later. Still later, about eleven o'clock, their mother would have her breakfast taken up.

He went into the kitchen.

"Let me have two pieces of toast and marmalade, rush, will you, Mathilde?"

She had been part of the household years before he was born. Short-legged and squat, she had, in spite of her sixty-four years, a young, fresh face, and it was her custom to grumble away all by herself in the kitchen.

She was the most solid member of the household, and when everything threatened to reach a state of total disorganization, she reestablished some kind of order.

He opened the refrigerator mechanically, looking for some leftover to nibble.

"Tell me what you want, but don't start picking around in all the dishes."

It was their daily little argument.

"Go and sit down at the table. I'll bring it in to you."

From his place, he could see a part of the garden, in particular the old linden tree for which he had a special affection. The house had been called "Two Lindens" from time immemorial. There was only one now, full of light and shade and of birds' song. Only a few leaves had begun to yellow.

The other linden tree, probably planted by his great-grandfather, had died long ago and had been replaced by birches.

No one would have thought they were in the center of Lausanne, in that steep street too narrow for two cars to pass. A low wall surrounded the property, and the wrought-iron gate was never closed.

"What is there for lunch, Mathilde?"

"Veal casserole with noodles."

He ate quickly, looking now at the linden tree on his right, now at the wall half paneled in dark wood. Then, bareheaded, putting on only a well-worn suède jacket, he went to the garage at the end of the garden and took out his motorbike.

He had a social psychology course at eight o'clock and, at ten o'clock, a course in statistics.

He had decided to take his degree in sociology and was now in his third and last year. He hoped to go on to his doctorate after that.

At eleven o'clock he left Rue Charles-Vuillermet, behind the cathedral, where the courses in social sciences and psychology were given in the buildings of the law faculty.

Nothing had changed in the dining room, except that his and his father's cup had disappeared. His sister's place was still set.

He opened the kitchen door.

"Hasn't Odile come down?"

"I haven't seen or heard her."

His sister was like his mother. In the evenings she could not make up her mind to go to bed. Even when she did not go out, she hung around as late as possible, watching television in the drawing room, reading whatever came to hand, sometimes even comic strips, although she was over eighteen, and going to bed only when she was so tired she could scarcely stand.

Their mother read too, and both of them slept late in the morning. You had to wait until lunchtime to see them. Their father went to bed early, and now he was upstairs, in his study, working quietly. They hardly saw him, except at mealtimes. He had taken down a dividing wall on the second floor, transforming the attic into a vast library where he took his siesta after lunch on an old red sofa.

"There's a letter for you. I put it in your room."

Intrigued, he went upstairs and pushed open his door. The sun had moved around and was not shining on the same walls. He found the letter on his desk and was astonished to recognize his sister's handwriting. He opened it, vaguely worried. Odile had always been unpredictable, and one could expect anything from her.

According to the postmark, the letter had been mailed the evening before. Now, Odile had not been home for dinner that night. That was nothing unusual. She came and went as she pleased and she often came home at three in the morning.

He crossed the hall and opened his sister's bedroom

door. The bed had not been slept in. There was none of the usual disorder.

He returned to his own room, sat down in his armchair and read:

"My dear Bob,
"You will surprised to see this letter. No doubt you will find it when you come home for lunch, and I can imagine you examining the postmark with your eagle eye. Then you'll rush up to my room and find it empty. At that moment I will be far away."

It was one of his sister's habits to try to guess what people, particularly those in her own family, were going to do, and one had to admit that she was rarely wrong.

The handwriting was small and regular, but the number of downstrokes was erratic—there could be two or four for an *m*, and some letters were practically indecipherable. A *t*, for example, could be taken for an *i*.

When exactly had she written on these pages? The letter had been posted at six o'clock the previous evening. At the station? That was probable, since she said that when her brother read it she would already be far away. Now, leaving, for Odile, meant going to Paris, where she had been only four or five times, but which she considered the only place where she could possibly live.

Lausanne and other towns were for her some sort

of prisons which she put up with since she could do nothing else.

"I am very fond of you, Bob. You are the only person in the world I am sorry to be leaving. I wanted to kiss you good-by, but I was afraid I would get too emotional and burst into tears. Because, you know, it's a long, long journey I'm making, the longest that one can make.

"As for Mother and Daddy, I must confess that I don't particularly mind one way or the other, although perhaps Daddy doesn't deserve that.

"He's a good old dear who has organized things so that he can live in peace. I don't know if he has found any happiness that way, but he has achieved a kind of serenity.

"What I find touching in him is that we have never seen him drunk. He manages to drink so that he keeps more or less sober, and in the evening only one of us can tell that he has had his two bottles of Dôle.

"He must wait impatiently for the time for his next glass, constantly looking at the clock.

"Poor Daddy! And poor all of us! You're the only one who doesn't feel the weight of the house which is suffocating us, and I don't know how you do it. You must be born strong. If I'd been a boy, I would have left home long ago.

"You know by now that I have left for good, don't you? It isn't just an escapade and I haven't succumbed to a brainstorm. I have been thinking of this departure for a long time. A final departure. I am saying good-by not only to the house but to life, which has become more and more unbearable for me.

"I am useless. No one will be hurt by my disappearance. They will hardly notice it, except for you, and you have your work, which absorbs your attention. You're very lucky in that. Nothing interests me. Life is like slightly muddy water, neither cold nor hot, tepid water, like dishwater.

"There will be no scandal, for there will be no funeral either. I'll fix things so that my body is not found, or if it is, so that no one will be able to identify me.

"It will be enough to tell people that I have gone away without leaving any address.

"For some weeks, if not months, I have thought of many solutions, and there are several which seem to me to be acceptable. I have not yet chosen. I am going to give myself two or three days to decide.

"Daddy will be sad for a little while, but he is so accustomed to his selfish little life that he will soon take up his habits again.

"As for Mother, she's not concerned with appearances but with the family, and she will only sigh:

" 'And to think of all we've done for that child! I always said she wasn't normal.'

"I have often been tempted to talk to you as I am doing in this letter, but at the last moment I would keep quiet because I was afraid that you would think me ridiculous.

"All this has been going on for a long time, Bobby.

When I was a little girl I always felt ill at ease in the house and my reading showed me families that were real families.

"I was left to myself. I would hide myself in the garden or in the huge, dark drawing room where nobody goes except to watch television. Once, at the end of one of my moods, Mother asked me:

" 'Shall we go in to town, Odile?'

"I hated those trips, held by the hand as if I were on the end of a leash. She would meet women she knew and they would chat in the middle of the sidewalk while the passers-by bumped into me.

"She refused to buy me an ice-cream cone, because one doesn't eat those things in the street.

"I had to be very tidy, very clean, very well-behaved.

"I don't know how you managed to get them to leave you alone. Perhaps it has something to do with your being a boy.

"And the silent meals with, from time to time, a sentence that found no reply!

"You're a nice boy, Bob. I am sure that you will understand me, that you will forgive me. I seem to be only accusing others and to be putting all the weight of my decision on their shoulders. However, that isn't true. I realize that my real enemy is myself. You see, I don't feel at ease in life.

"As long as I can remember, I have considered myself different from my friends. That is perhaps pride. I don't know. I should have had some other kind of life, but I am the first to admit I don't know what kind.

"That is why I have tried a little of everything and why in the end, though I'm past eighteen, I know nothing. I haven't even the most elementary diploma that would allow me to take up a career if I should find one I wanted.

"If I hang about in the evenings, as late as possible, watching television or reading, it is because I am afraid to be alone with myself.

"I think too much about myself, but I can't help it.

"I had some friends at high school. Quite frankly, I didn't like them and after quite a short time they would get on my nerves.

" 'You must invite So-and-So or So-and-So,' Mother was always saying.

"Invite them to do what? They didn't have the same interests as I did. Their chatter, their senseless giggling, seemed juvenile to me.

"I am tired of writing and yet I want so much to explain everything to you. Then there would be at least one person who would not think of me as a weather vane, shifting constantly, or as if I were ill.

"Mathilde has told me that I was never a real child, that when I was very small I behaved like a grownup, and that all I wanted was to be alone. They would find me sitting on the branch of a tree, at the far end of the garden, or even in the cellar.

" 'What are you doing there?' they would ask.

"I would look at them without answering. What could I have answered?

"I would become very interested in a friend at school. I would invite her to the house, and after a few weeks I wouldn't be able to stand her any more.

"When I went to a friend's, for a birthday party, for example, I would feel ill at ease in an apartment so different from our house, where the mother would try to amuse us.

" 'What are you thinking about, Odile?'

" 'Nothing, madame.'

"I was polite. I had been taught to be polite. Good morning, monsieur. Good morning, madame. Thank you, monsieur.

"Heaven only knows how many times I have said thank you in my life!

"I really must decide to finish this letter. You have guessed that I have gone to Paris, haven't you? It is the best place to disappear.

"I don't want you to feel sorry for me. Since I have made up my mind, I don't feel unhappy any more. It will be a bad moment to go through, but very short, shorter than going to the dentist.

"And afterward I shall be free. Free of myself, the person who has tortured me, perhaps without reason.

"Are you tired of reading my letter by now? I have the feeling that I am writing to you as if I were the center of the world. Do you understand me, or do you think me conceited? I am stupid to ask you that question, since I shall never know the answer.

"Well, my dear Bob, don't think about that any more, now my decision is made. And don't mourn for me. It would be more painful for me to go on living than to go away.

"When you see Uncle Arthur, tell him I don't blame him. It isn't his fault. I have thought about it and I have finally understood that it was I who provoked him. It's true, I was only fifteen. It's true that he didn't go all the way. I didn't know that. It was only later that I understood.

"I haven't been lucky with men. I say men because I have never been interested in boys of my own age. Was I wrong about that? They didn't interest me.

"It doesn't matter.

"You see, my great discovery is that I have never done anything for anyone. I blamed everything on other people. Then, little by little, I asked myself questions.

"Even when I happened to do something generous, it was as if I were looking at myself in the mirror to watch myself making a handsome gesture.

"Why, then, can't I finish this letter? I think it is because the most important part is missing, that all I have been saying to you isn't what really matters.

"When I began I thought that it would be easy, that I only had to let my pen run over the paper without taking the time to think.

"Will you understand? I hope so, even though I shan't know. Destroy this letter. Don't show it to Daddy, or to Mother. After all, they've only done what they could, both of them.

"I shall think about you a lot, Bob, in what's left to me of time, your kindness, your nice, open smile. You are a well-balanced boy who knows what he wants and who will get it. You will get married. You will have children. I only hope that you don't stay at Two Lindens. I think that the lives that have been lived there, one after another, have left an oppressive atmosphere.

"Well, that's that! So once more I am going off in another direction. It is time I finished. I give you a big kiss on your always stubbly cheeks, dear Bob. Soon you will be smiling again, or, better, you will laugh your usual loud laugh.

"Bye-bye!

"Your idiot sister,

"Odile"

He stayed there for a long time, motionless, the sheets of paper in his hand. When he heard steps on the stairs, he shoved them into his pocket.

"Lunch is served, Bob."

She did not say "monsieur," any more than she said "mademoiselle" to his sister. She was the one who had in fact brought them up, and they had always called her *tu* since they were children.

"Is my father down?"

"It's half past twelve."

"And my mother?"

"She's at the table."

He kissed them both on the forehead, bending his long, lean figure over them. He had one of those loosely knit bodies which gave him the appearance of having the suppleness of an acrobat.

"Isn't your sister coming down?"

"She isn't in her room."

"Did she say where she was going?"

His mother, a very dark woman, wore a blue silk dressing gown. Before she started her hors d'oeuvre, she finished her cigarette. She smoked from the moment she got up until the time she went to bed, and at the end of the day her fingers trembled because of it.

His father had gray hair, almost white, which accentuated the youthful appearance of his face.

"She didn't say anything to me, but she left me a letter."

Marthe Pointet's eyes were almost black, and her look was penetrating.

"Aren't you going to show it to us?"

"I think I must have torn it up. She just says that she's going to Paris and that she prefers not to leave any address."

"Did you hear that, Albert?"

"When did she go?"

"As far as I can tell, last evening, on the Trans European Express at six thirteen."

"Do you think she was alone?"

"I imagine so."

"There isn't a man behind all this?"

"I don't have that impression."

The father looked at his plate without saying a word.

"All the same, it's quite unthinkable!" cried Marthe Pointet, her voice sharp. "Imagine a girl of only just eighteen going off without saying a thing to her family. Has she got any money?"

"I think she had been saving what she got for Christmas and her birthdays."

"She doesn't say when she is coming back?"

"No."

"I can hardly believe it. If my friends guess about it, they would wonder what kind of family I have brought up."

She turned to her husband.

"And you, you're not saying anything. You're eating!"

"What could I say?"

"Anything, but don't be so indifferent. It's our daughter, after all."

"I know."

"I wonder if we ought to inform the police."

"That wouldn't do any good. If she wants to disappear . . ."

"What do you mean, disappear?"

"Make her life apart from us . . ."

"And why should she, can you tell me that?"

"Probably because she's fed up."

"Fed up with what?"

"I don't know . . . She's young. She's going ahead with her own life."

The meal had dragged on to its end with silence around the oval table, where, opposite Bob, his sister's luncheon things had not been removed. Hardly had she swallowed her last mouthful when Marthe Pointet lit a cigarette while her husband got up, sighing, as if to do so were a painful exercise.

In fact, apart from his morning walk in Mon Repos Park, he took no physical exercise, and the Dôle wine did nothing to make him thinner. He was going to go up to his room. In that household they were only together at mealtimes, then each person went about his own business.

"Are you going out?" Bob asked his mother.

"No. I have a bridge party here at four o'clock."

That was what she devoted the greatest part of her days to. She had friends who came to Two Lindens, or to whose houses she went in her turn. They started with tea and cakes, then, toward half past five, these good ladies turned to whisky.

"Do you know if she has taken anything with her?" Albert Pointet asked, his hand on the doorknob.

"I didn't see the blue suitcase she was given last Christmas. Her toilet case isn't there either."

"Any clothes?"

"I don't think there's anything missing, except her camel-hair coat. She never wanted to wear that. She found it too formal."

"I shan't say anything to my friends about her going," said Marthe. "There's no point in having everyone gossiping about it just now. Since she's certainly going to come back some day or other . . ."

"I don't think so," answered Bob.

"What makes you say that?"

"It's just the impression I have."

His sister's letter was certainly in her usual style, and Odile was not averse to dramatizing herself. It was not the first time she had spoken of suicide, but this time the tone was different.

Albert Pointet started up the stairs. His wife followed him directly, and Bob, standing in front of the window, looked at the old linden tree that he had called "his" tree when he was a boy because he used to climb up and sit in the highest branches.

He heard Mathilde, who was clearing the table.

"Why didn't you tell the truth?"

"The truth?"

"That she left last evening and that she sent you a letter through the mail. I know her well, and she didn't just send you a note. You had a long letter, didn't you?"

"Yes."

"Aren't you going to show it to them?"

"No."

"Why not?"

"Because she talks about them and what she says wouldn't make them very happy."

"Do you really think she has gone to Paris?"

"I think so. I could be wrong."

"What is she going to do there?"

"I don't know. What comes out in the letter is that she wants to disappear completely. That may mean that she is thinking of committing suicide. That reminds me, I want to check something."

He took the stairs four by four and went into his parents' bathroom, where the medicine cabinet was. Everyone in the house, now that the children were grown up, came and took what he wanted from it as he wished. Bob looked carefully at the bottles of tablets, and what he had suspected a moment ago was shown to be so in fact: the bottle of sleeping pills had disappeared.

He went back into his sister's room, where her guitar was in its place in a corner and several stuffed animals dating from her childhood sat on some shelves. In the wardrobe there were very few skirts, but half a dozen pairs of slacks. The jacket, exactly the same as his, had disappeared.

It was Wednesday. The school and the *lycée* were closed in the afternoon. He went down to the drawing room, where the telephone was, and rang the Duprés' house.

"Hello, madame. This is Bob Pointet. May I speak to Jeanne, please?"

At school, the Béthusy high school, she had been in the same class as Odile for five years and they saw a lot of each other, going to each other's houses. It wasn't a regular thing. It depended on Odile's mood. For weeks, or months, she would consider Jeanne her best friend and then, suddenly, wouldn't want to speak to her any more. Now Jeanne Dupré was nineteen and in her last year at the *lycée*. She was an open, gay girl, her eyes an almost transparent blue.

"Hello. Is that you, Bob?"

"Yes."

"What are you doing these days?"

"Working, as usual. I wanted to ask you if you had seen my sister in the last few days?"

"Well, you know, since she left school . . ."

"Yes, I know."

She did not see her old friends, girls or boys, willingly. As far as she was concerned, they had remained children. She had joined new groups that frequented the less reputable bars in the town.

"Wait . . . About a week ago I met her on the Rue de Bourg, and she insisted on buying me an ice cream."

"How was she?"

"You want me to tell you the truth, don't you? I thought she was nervous and a bit odd. She asked me what I was going to do after the *lycée*. I said I wanted to study pharmacy.

" 'Do you really think you'll enjoy that?' she asked me ironically.

" 'Why not? It's a good career for a woman, and I hope I may have my own business someday.'

" 'Well, I wish you the best of luck. And for you to meet a handsome pharmacist! Then you could have little pharmacists . . .' "

"I know that mood."

"So do I. However, I asked her why she seemed so bitter. She seized me by the arm.

" 'Don't pay any attention to me. I'm in the middle of making a big decision. You'll hear about it soon.'

" 'You're not happy.'

" 'I have never been happy.'

" 'I can remember the day when you were the life and soul of the party.'

" 'Because I was playing a part.'

" 'You're playing a part now too, aren't you?'

" 'No. This time it's serious. But I don't want to say any more about it. I'm glad I ran into you. I used to be horrible to you, but I am really very fond of you. You'll have a nice life, well organized, with your work, your husband, your children. You won't ask yourself any questions . . .'

"Well, Bob, that's more or less what she said to me. Her face looked drawn. She told me that she could never get to sleep before early in the morning."

"I suppose she was wearing slacks and her jacket?"

"Yes."

"Do you remember what color her slacks were?"

"Yes. Rust-colored."

Now, his sister had the habit of wearing the same clothes for two or three weeks, and the rust-colored slacks, which Bob hadn't thought of, were not in her wardrobe.

"Be a good girl and don't mention this telephone call to anyone. She wouldn't be pleased if she learned I'd been asking you questions."

"What are you afraid of, Bob?"

"What about you?"

"I'm wondering if we're thinking the same thing."

"She has some idea of suicide . . ."

"You're not telling me anything new. She thought about that at school, but I thought it was part of the role she was playing. Because she was playing a part . . . It wasn't always the same one. She needed people to pay attention to her. She needed them to admire her, too. And, in fact, she was more intelligent than we were."

"Can your mother hear you?"

"No. She went out to do her shopping when you called up. I'm alone in the house. My two brothers are with neighbors.

"What are you going to do?"

"I'm going to Paris. Do you know if any of the people she's been going around with lately live in Paris?"

"I know almost none of her new friends. My father and mother let me go to parties on condition that they are at the homes of people they know."

She had been in love with him at one time, and they had exchanged a few kisses and superficial caresses. Jeanne Dupré's voice was nostalgic, as if she had not yet forgotten.

"Good luck, Bob."

"Thank you, Jeanne. All the best . . ."

He hung up and wondered whom he could call next. All his sister's old friends would have less to tell him than Jeanne, for Odile had deliberately lost touch with them.

There was one boy she had been involved with for a time, Alex Carus, the son of Doctor Carus on Avenue de Rumine. Bob had been to his house only once, and had been impressed by his friend's bedroom, a former artist's studio.

He called him and was lucky enough to find him at home. It was true that it was mostly in the evenings and late at night that Alex went out.

"This is Bob . . ."

"Bob Pointet?"

"Yes."

"What are you doing with yourself, and to what do I owe this telephone call? We haven't seen each other for more than three years."

He was nineteen, like most of Odile's friends. For a while, at the Béthusy high school, they talked of "Odile's crowd." He too had given up his studies. He played several musical instruments, and he had formed a small group with other young people.

"Have you seen much of my sister lately?"

"I saw her one night in the Brasserie de l'Ours, where I was having a snack with some friends of mine. She was eating, too, at another table. I asked her to join us, but she didn't want to."

"How was she?"

"Not exactly forthcoming. I asked her if she still played the guitar, because she could have joined our group . . . I'm not saying we're a great group, but we have had several public engagements and a reputable company in Geneva has promised to make a record of our music. She told me she hadn't touched her guitar for over a year."

"Is that all?"

"My friends were waiting for me. I didn't have anything to say to her.

" 'Ciao!'

" 'Ciao!'

"She left a little later, alone, and there was something listless in the way she moved."

"Thanks."

"Why are you asking me these questions?"

"Because she has gone to Paris without letting anybody know."

"She's had that idea in her head for a long time. Whenever anyone talked about the future, it was always Paris for her. She couldn't understand how one could live in Lausanne, and she was quite contemptuous of those who meant to stay here."

"Thank you. I'm sorry to have bothered you."

"I'm expecting my friends in a quarter of an hour for a rehearsal."

"Doesn't your father mind the noise you make?"

"I'm at the other end of the apartment."

Bob hung up and looked around him. It was the darkest room in the house, and Odile was quite right in saying that it wasn't cheerful.

Their grandfather, Urbain Pointet, had been Professor of Law for thirty-five years. The house where the family lived now had been his. Bob's father and mother had come to live there at the professor's request, after the death of his wife.

He had a handsome head of hair, a well-trimmed beard, at first a pale gray and then gleaming white. What was now the big drawing room had then been his study and library. Here, too, paneling covered part of the walls and the rest was covered in an embossed paper imitating cordovan leather.

The bookshelves, which went from floor to ceiling, contained thousands of books and bound journals, and no one had ever dared to touch them.

Urbain Pointet, who had been a highly regarded figure in the community, had died ten years ago but instead of taking over his study, Bob's father had continued to work in his attic, which he found more congenial.

The door opened. Mathilde came in and set up the bridge table, then went to one of the cupboards to get out the cards and score-pads.

"What are you doing in here, Bob?"

"I was telephoning."

"Did you find out anything?"

"Nothing interesting. Only that she has been planning this departure for a long time."

"Are you going to Paris?"

"I'm going up to talk to Father about it."

"Where do you think you'll find her among millions of people?"

"She has at least one friend there, or anyway it's a friend of mine whom she had a crush on. She has a girl friend there too, Emilienne. I know her address. As a last resort, there's the police."

"Wouldn't you hesitate before going to the police?"

"No. I can tell you, at least—I am scared about her."

"So am I. Poor little thing! It's not her fault, you know . . ."

"I know that very well, and I would be happier if I could find her . . ."

Some minutes later he knocked at the attic door. A voice grumbled:

"Come in!"

His father must have recognized his footsteps on the stairs. He too had a beard, but it was red and badly trimmed. He had bushy eyebrows, and tufts of hair stuck out from his ears.

He was seated in front of the huge table that he used as a desk. It was always covered with books, journals, and notebooks.

Could one say that his professional life had been a failure? When he had taken his doctorate in History, he had probably thought of teaching, perhaps of doing research.

Had he been disillusioned, or had he decided to choose the easier way?

He wrote thick books which were clamored for by the Paris publishers, for they all sold in impressive numbers. He wrote one book a year on the average, choosing his subject carefully to appeal to a wide public.

They were not really historical novels, but more what one might call intimate history. He would bring to life a little-known conspiracy, or he would track down the list of mistresses of a king or some noted personage.

He wrote in a big, clear, firm hand, with no trace of nervousness or fatigue. He knew the number of pages he must cover each day, and he did it conscientiously, rewarding himself with a glass of red wine every hour on the hour.

"Do you want to talk to me about your sister?"

"Not especially."

"Are there things you prefer not to say in front of your mother?"

"Yes. It's quite serious. She threatens to commit suicide, and this time I think she is capable of it."

His father held out his hand.

"May I read her letter?"

"I have destroyed it."

"Why?"

"Because it said things that were too personal."

"I imagine she was speaking of your mother and me."

Bob was very fond of his father, and could have been his friend if there had been any place for such a thing in Albert Pointet's too well-regulated life. Behind his unkempt appearance he hid a sharp intelligence, but he rarely showed it.

He sighed.

"I was wrong to accept my father's invitation to come and live here with my family when he became a widower. It is an old people's house, and I can understand that young people might rebel against it."

"I don't think that is the real reason . . ."

"I spend all day in this untidy attic, taking a glass of wine every hour. At half past nine I am in bed, but I am up again at half past five, all alone in the house.

"The only time I go out is to go to the university library or to go to Paris to see one of my publishers.

"Your mother spends a good half of her time in bed, and her principal occupation is playing bridge. By the way, have her friends arrived?"

"They hadn't, a few minutes ago."

"Sometimes I wonder if she's quite normal, or whatever it is that people say. You heard her at lunch—no emotion, her only reaction was that the news would get around, that her friends would find out. Sit down, son."

He lit a cigar, and asked Bob:

"Do you want one?"

"No, thank you."

"What did you come for?"

Usually he came up to the attic because he needed money. Indirectly, that was the reason again.

"I am going to Paris."

"Do you think you will find her?"

"I won't lose anything by trying. I know two or three people with whom she may have got, or may still get, in touch."

"It's probably not a bad idea. You are afraid, aren't you?"

"Yes."

"Did she say anything about it to you?"

"About dying? Yes."

"Don't say anything about that to your mother. I share your fear . . ."

He took a fat wallet out of his trousers pocket and counted out hundred-franc notes.

"Here's five hundred. If you need more just send me a telegram. When are you leaving?"

"On the T.E.E. at six thirteen."

His father leaned his head forward as usual, and Bob kissed him on the forehead.

"Will you be staying on Rue Gay-Lussac?"

It was there, to the Hôtel Mercator, that Bob, like his father, usually went. It was in the heart of the Latin Quarter, close to the Sorbonne and the Luxembourg Gardens. The proprietor was no longer Merca-

tor, and had probably not been so for several genera-
tions, but a man whose name went well with his plump
face and round body: Monsieur Bedon.

"If you don't hear from me it's because I haven't
any news for you."

His father followed him with his eyes as far as the
door, looked at his watch, and reached out for the bottle. It was three minutes past the hour.

Chapter 2

Bob had taken only a small suitcase which held, apart from a change of linen, a pair of flannel slacks and a pair of shoes for changing into in case he should be caught in a heavy shower.

When he left the house he avoided the drawing room, where his mother's friends could be heard chattering, and so he did not say good-by to her. Instead, he went into the kitchen.

"I knew you would go," Mathilde said. "Do try everything to find her, Bob. I don't know why, but I have the feeling that she's in real danger. I have felt for a long time that there was something wrong with her state of mind."

He went out of the garden and appeared to say good-by to his tree, into which the setting sun was sending reddish reflections. The same reddish light could be seen on the surface of the lake beyond the town.

He strode down the steep street, crossed Mon Repos Park, and found a taxi.

"To the station, please."

He drowsed through most of the journey. In the dining car, he asked the headwaiter:

"Were you on this run yesterday?"

"Yes, monsieur."

"Did you notice a very young girl who seemed upset or nervous?"

"We see so many people, you know . . ."

He showed him a photograph of his sister.

"I think she sat in that corner. A table for two. She came in alone, but the person opposite her wasn't long in speaking to her, and they left the dining car together."

"What kind of man?"

"A gentleman. Still quite young. In his forties . . ."

In Paris he took a taxi to Rue Gay-Lussac. The building was the smallest in the street, only three floors, squeezed in between houses of five and six floors. On the other side of the desk a door was open, and he could see the proprietor, Monsieur Bedon, leaning over a pile of papers.

"Goodness, Monsieur Bob! What good wind blows you in here?"

"More of an ill wind. Before anything else, tell me if my sister is here by any chance."

"No. It's almost six months now since she has been here."

"Did you notice anything odd on her last visit?"

"She stayed for three days . . ."

"I know that."

"She went out the first evening, immediately after taking her suitcase upstairs, and she told me she was going out for a bit of air. In fact, I can tell you this, she didn't come back until about four in the morning."

"How did she seem?"

"Very well, apparently. It was old Victor who gave her her key. They chatted for quite a while. Is she in Paris?"

"Probably."

"I'm surprised that she hasn't come to stay here as usual."

Monsieur Bedon frowned.

"Are you here to look for her?"

"More or less. She left home without any warning."

"She is certainly a very independent young lady."

"Did she come back in just as late, the two other nights she spent in Paris?"

"I must admit that she did."

"Did that happen the other times she came?"

"Never three nights in a row. She practically never went out in the daytime. She had sandwiches taken up at two in the afternoon, then she must have gone back to sleep. She didn't put her nose out of doors until dinnertime."

"Thank you, Monsieur Bedon."

The proprietor took down a key from the rack and handed it to him.

"It's number 12, the room you had last time."

He recognized the room, with its flowered wallpaper, its brass bedstead, and its big mirrored wardrobe.

As his sister had done six months previously, he went downstairs again right away, waved to the proprietor, and went toward Boulevard Saint-Germain. What Monsieur Bedon had just told him about Odile's last stay in Paris had reminded him of something she had said.

"I've found a fabulous *boîte* in Saint-Germain-des-Prés. There are only five musicians, but they manage to create a marvelous atmosphere. It's very small. It's called Le Cannibale."

That was where he was heading, on the off chance. He had some difficulty in finding the sign and the stair that led down into a basement where one could hear Pop music.

It was not big, in fact. The room must have been capable of holding about thirty people, but for the moment it was only half full. On a narrow stage were five musicians with very long hair, and the guitarist had the longest hair of all.

"Are you alone?" asked the proprietor in a strong Swedish accent.

"Yes."

"That doesn't matter. Sit down at this table. What's your drink?"

"A Scotch."

He was served by a pretty girl wearing the shortest skirt he had ever seen.

Most of the people were couples, lovers, some of whom were dancing on a tiny dance floor.

"Tell me, is this the same orchestra that was here six months ago?"

"Yes, monsieur. They've been here for almost a year now. They're good, aren't they?"

"Yes, they are."

He waited for half an hour until the music stopped. Three of the musicians stayed where they were and had a cigarette. One of them went to the bar and one went outside. It was the guitarist. Bob followed him out onto the sidewalk, where the man was getting a breath of air.

He had a bit of a blond beard, not much, and he seemed very young, still a boy.

"Cigarette?"

The guitarist took one.

"Thank you."

"Do you often have unaccompanied women in the *boîte*?"

"Not very often. And never professionals. The proprietor won't allow that. It's funny, but he's a real prude in his way."

"I'd like to know if you recognize this face."

He showed him Odile's photograph which his companion took over to a gas lamp to study.

When he handed back the photograph he seemed hesitant.

"What is she to you?" he asked.

"She's my sister. But don't worry. She has complete freedom, and I know about most of her affairs."

"Are you sure?"

"Yes."

"Has she spoken to you about me?"

"Not about you, but about Le Cannibale. You have slept with her, haven't you?"

"Yes."

"It was she who spoke to you first, wasn't it?"

"Yes."

"I know my sister."

"She wanted to talk about the guitar. She plays too."

"Yes, she used to play.

"What else did she tell you?"

"That she lived in Lausanne, in an old house dating back to her great-grandfather, and that she was bored to death there. I asked her why she didn't come to Paris to live, and she said that she didn't have any money or any profession.

" 'All I could do,' she sighed, 'would be to stand behind a counter in one of the department stores.' "

"Did she stay here until you closed?"

"Yes."

"And she went home with you?"

Odile would not have dared to take anyone to the Hôtel Mercator.

"If one can call it a home. I have a room, badly furnished and not very nice, in a lodginghouse on Rue Mouffetard."

"She went there with you."

"Yes. We didn't only make love. She talked a lot. I must admit she had had two or three drinks."

"What did she talk about?"

"About herself. She envied me having a profession, even if I earned very little. She was sorry she had given up the guitar.

" 'It's like that with everything,' she sighed. 'I begin something with enthusiasm and I think that I am saved at last, that I have found the right thing for me. Then, one month or six months later, I feel as if I were struggling in a vacuum. Nothing exists any more. I am sick of myself . . .' "

"I know her well and she has often said the same things to me."

"You know, she's not really interested in sex."

"I've always imagined that."

"She wants her partner to have pleasure through her, but she herself doesn't have any . . . I must go down now. There's another break in half an hour."

Bob sat down again at the table and ordered another drink.

"You've never been here before?" asked the proprietor.

"No. My sister has been here several times, some time ago."

He showed him the photograph and the man with the Scandinavian accent recognized her.

"A pretty girl. She stayed in her corner, the left-hand corner, near the orchestra, for hours. She only left at closing time . . . How old is she, really?"

"When you knew her, she wasn't yet eighteen. She is now."

"Didn't she come to Paris with you?"

"No. She came alone and I am looking for her."

The proprietor looked automatically at the guitarist, and Bob hastened to say:

"I know. I've just been talking to him, outside."

"Doesn't he know anything?"

"He hasn't seen her this trip. She must have got here last night."

"I haven't seen her either. You seem worried."

"I am. When she left home she was very depressed. In a letter she left me, she talked about putting an end to it all."

"In that case, there isn't much chance she'll come here."

"That's true. Did she tell you anything about herself?"

"No. I just asked her to dance, twice, and she accepted both times."

Half an hour later, the guitarist came to sit down at his table.

"A Scotch?"

"No. A beer. I'm hot . . . A beer, Lucienne."

"And another whisky."

"Was the boss able to tell you anything interesting?"

"No. He danced with her, but she hardly spoke to him. Do you think he has slept with her?"

"No, he doesn't do that sort of thing . . . And besides, Lucienne wouldn't let him. That's been going on for more than a year, the two of them."

"Can you think of anything, even something she said by chance, that could put me on my sister's tracks?"

"Do you want to take her back to Lausanne?"

"Not necessarily. If I found her, I'm not even sure I would tell my parents. I'm looking for her to stop her from making an irreparable mistake."

"She's a very intelligent girl, and she has real insight into herself."

"I know."

"She makes herself very unhappy. She came three evenings in a row."

"Did you go to Rue Mouffetard all three evenings?"

"I couldn't go to her hotel, that hotel with the funny name . . ."

"Mercator."

"Yes. It seems all the family goes there. She even went there when she was a little girl."

"That's true."

"She's both a very complicated and a very simple person. Very candid. She didn't know me, yet right from the first evening she told me things that one would only tell an old friend. The second night, she asked me to take the guitar home. She stretched out on the bed, quite naked, and she wanted me to play for her alone. That shows a romantic character, doesn't it?"

Bob did not answer. He was thinking, trying to put in order the information he had gathered in that way.

"Here's to you."

"And you."

"She didn't say anything to you about any friend, boy or girl, she might have in Paris?"

"She mentioned a boy, but he was more your friend than hers."

"Lucien Denge?"

"I don't know his name. I only know he does something in films."

"That's he. Has she slept with him too?"

"She didn't say. She also mentioned a girl who was studying art history."

"Emilienne?"

"That could well be the name she said."

And the musician added, a little embarrassed:

"I'm sorry about what happened . . . I swear I didn't have that in mind . . . I'm not putting the blame on her, but I was quite surprised . . . I must get back to work. Thanks for the beer."

He held out his hand.

"My name is Christian Vermeulen. I'm from Roubaix. I threw up everything, too, to come to Paris."

His smile was open, a little shy.

"I hope we'll meet again. And I hope you find her.

If she comes in here or to my place, I'll give you a ring. The Hôtel Mercator, you said?"

"Yes, on Rue Gay-Lussac."

Bob called Lucienne so that he could pay the bill. The proprietor shook hands with him.

"Good luck."

No one thought he was a fool, and the people here, at least, thought well of Odile.

He walked back to the hotel. Most certainly the picture of his sister that he was building up was becoming clearer and clearer. He was beginning to realize that he had not really known her. And yet the two of them got on very well. Was it impossible to know a member of one's family really well?

He imagined her naked on the bed in the Rue Mouffetard room, having the guitar played to her and listening, staring at the ceiling.

He knew that she had had several lovers, and he had suspected that she was frigid.

What she wanted was to talk, to talk to someone who did not know her and who would listen to her with interest.

She had no confidence in herself. Or rather, that depended on the occasion. Sometimes she had too much and she went too far. She needed to find a way of exteriorizing herself, of affirming her personality, of showing that she was an exceptional girl.

After that would come the crisis of humility, as when she had written the letter she had sent to him.

Back in his room, he read it again. He was more moved than he had been the first time, because of what the musician had told him.

There were five million human beings around him, and he was looking for only one, a young girl who did not want to be found, who was perhaps already dead.

Why did she not want anyone to find her body? Wasn't it a sort of challenge? And how did she think she would manage it?

He finally went to sleep. When he woke, in the middle of the morning, a thin, yellowish fog lay over the city. He was shaving when the phone rang.

He rushed to it, hoping God knows what, but it was his father who was at the other end.

"I don't suppose you have any news?"

"No. But I know where she spent the three evenings on her last trip to Paris."

"Where?"

"In a nightspot on Boulevard Saint-Germain."

"Alone?"

"She went there alone and she met one of the musicians."

"I can guess what happened."

"Yes."

"Does he not know anything?"

"No. He talked to me a lot about her. The proprietor of the *boîte* did too."

"What are you going to do?"

"Go on questioning people. There are two or three

people in Paris whom she used to know. She may have got in touch with one of them."

"I hope so. Keep me in the picture. I haven't been able to work this morning. I am alone in my attic, kicking my heels."

"I'll call you soon."

"Yes, soon. Preferably with good news."

Bob was surprised. He was suddenly discovering a father who was different from the image he had always had of him. He remembered what his sister had said to him several times.

"Daddy is an old egoist who only thinks about his work and his wine. As for Mother, she's completely turned in on herself."

But now, his father had just telephoned him, an act that had made him go downstairs to the drawing room, since that was where the only telephone in the house was. He had spoken many times of having an extension put in his study, but he had never had it done.

One could tell that he was worried and depressed.

It was only Odile who treated him as an old man, because of her own youth. Actually he had only just turned fifty and was in the prime of life.

Bob did not have Emilienne's address. She was more his sister's friend than his. He went to the Sorbonne, to the office. It was not an easy task. The first people he dealt with knew nothing about her.

"What course is she taking?"

"Art History."

"Go to Room 21."

In Room 21 they looked at him suspiciously.

"Is she a relative of yours?"

"No. She's a friend of my sister's."

"And why do you want her address?"

"To help me find my sister."

"Has she disappeared?"

"Yes."

"Of her own accord?"

"Yes."

"How old is she?"

"Eighteen."

"Where are you from?"

"From Lausanne."

"And your sister has run away to come to Paris. Has she been here before?"

"Several times, but that was with my parents' knowledge."

"I'll see what I can do."

He went into another room. The door was open, but he spoke in a low voice and Bob did not hear what he said. When he came back after a long time, he said:

"Just a moment."

Opening a metal filing cabinet full of pink cards, he eventually picked one out.

"Emilienne Lhote, Avenue de la Sallaz?"

"That's right."

"Her address in Paris is Hôtel de la Néva, Rue des Ecoles."

"Thank you."

"Do you know what time she finishes her classes?"

"I'm not worried about that."

The hotel was really a family pension in the grounds of what must have been a vast mansion. The walls were painted white, and there were green shutters, as if it were in the country. A bench on each side of the door completed the illusion.

At the moment when Bob arrived the sun was shining full on the front of the building and the door was open. A broad, big-breasted girl was on her knees in the corridor, washing the floor.

"Would you happen to know if Mademoiselle Lhote is in her room?"

"Who did you say?"

"Mademoiselle Lhote . . . Emilienne Lhote."

"I know Mademoiselle Emilienne, but I don't know if she is upstairs. She doesn't keep the same hours every day. I'll call the landlady."

She came from the end of the corridor, wiping her hands on her gingham apron.

"Do you want to see Mademoiselle Emilienne?"

"Yes."

"She isn't in just now. I give my lodgers breakfast, and then dinner at eight o'clock. As for lunch, they fix it up themselves near where their work is. Are you a member of her family?"

"No. My sister and I went to the same school she did, in Lausanne, and we were friends."

Short and fat, the landlady made him think of Mathilde as she had been ten years before.

"You wouldn't know at about what time I would have the best chance of finding her in?"

"She usually comes in quite early, about half past six or seven."

"I'll come back then. Would you know if she had a visit from a girl yesterday?"

"I didn't see anybody, but I might well have been in the kitchen."

"Thank you."

He stepped carefully across the soapy water that had spread over the entire corridor and soon found himself outside again. He would come back, anyway. He knew that his sister had quarreled at one time with Emilienne, but they had made it up again later. Odile had quarreled with everyone in her class and with all the girls she used to go around with.

Bob had never had passionate friendships. He had never fallen madly for anyone. At school, and then at the *lycée*, he had had several friends, but he never saw them out of class. He knew his sister's friends better, because they came to the house and they played various instruments together. He had gone out with some of them, although they were much younger than he was. He didn't remember having gone out with Emilienne, a tall, thin, bony girl whose nose was too long.

He walked toward Rue de la Seine and found the shabby hotel where Lucien Denge lived. At the left of the door was the usual marbled sign saying:

Residential Hotel
Rooms let by the day,
by the week, and by the month

There was a window in the hall, giving on to a small room where one could see a roll-top desk, a board with keys hanging on it, and a shapeless arm-chair. An enormous woman, her bare legs swollen, her feet in red slippers, was reading the paper.

"Excuse me, madame. I would like to see Monsieur Denge, please."

"He isn't in."

"But he does still live here?"

"Of course. He wouldn't find as cheap a room with running hot and cold water anywhere else."

"You don't know when he'll be in?"

"At the moment he's making a film somewhere around Paris, possibly in the suburbs. They're doing what they call exterior shots. So they work irregular hours."

"Does he have dinner here?"

"No. He usually eats in a little place on Rue de Buci. But when he's shooting, he most often eats with the others."

"When do you think I'd be likely to find him?"

"I don't know . . . If all goes well, about ten o'clock . . . If he has a drink he'll have several and he's not likely to be back before midnight."

"Thank you."

"You're not here on behalf of his parents, are you?"

"Why? Is he afraid they'll visit him?"

"He's always afraid they'll come and look for him. You'd hardly know he was of age, he's so terrified of his mother. It seems she's a formidable woman."

The Denges lived in the Tunnel district of Lausanne. He had four sisters a lot younger than he was, all of them at school. Their father was a cashier in the Swiss Bank Association. Bob had seen him. He looked pleasant, if a little starchy. As for the mother, he had never caught sight of her.

He gave himself until the next day before telling the police. He knew there was a special department assigned to the search for missing persons on behalf of their families. As he was passing a police station, he went in and, leaning on a sort of counter, waited his turn. He was astonished to find the rooms bright and clean, the walls freshly painted.

"Have you got an appointment?"

"No. I wanted some information. When a person has disappeared, what department does one consult?"

"Is it a member of your family?"

"My sister."

"She isn't of age?"

"No. She is eighteen."

"How long ago did she disappear?"

"Two days ago."

"Maybe she's just gone off for a few days."

"She has never done that before."

"Well, anyway, this isn't the right spot. You will find the Bureau of Missing Persons at 11 Rue des Ursins, in the fourth *arrondissement*. It's in the same building as the Department of Health and Public Safety. Ask for Room 4."

He only had to cross the Seine. It was near the Quai aux Fleurs, but he didn't dare set the police in action yet. He preferred to try all he could do himself first, and then to telephone his father.

He spent an hour reading the paper at an outdoor café on Boulevard Saint-Germain, since it was still warm. Then he walked for a while and finally went into a movie house, for want of anything better to do.

When he went back to the pension, a little before seven o'clock, the woman asked him:

"What is your name?"

"Bob. Bob Pointet."

"Just a moment."

And, drawing her skirts about her, she started up the stairs. When she returned, she announced:

"She's coming down right away. Come this way."

They went through a dining room, where six or seven places were set about a round table, and went into a drawing room that smelled almost of the country, a spicy smell, in any case.

He was not welcomed with open arms. When Emilienne came in, she looked at him curiously, coldly.

"I understand you want to see me."

"Yes. You were one of Odile's friends."

"You know very well that Odile didn't have any friends."

"You haven't seen her recently?"

"The last time we met was over a year ago, on the Rue de Bourg."

"She hasn't tried to see you here, in Paris?"

"If she had asked for me, someone would have told me. Am I to understand she has disappeared?"

"Yes."

"You wouldn't have a cigarette, would you?"

He lit it for her, then lit one himself and sat down in one of the green rep armchairs.

She sat down opposite him.

"When did this happen?"

"Two days ago."

"Are you sure she's in Paris?"

"Where else?"

"She'll come back one of these days. All she wants is to draw attention to herself, as usual. She has never accepted the fact that she is a girl like other girls."

"I know. But I am still worried. She is desperate. She wants to disappear completely."

"Listen, Bob. Try to look at things a bit coldly. If she is desperate enough to commit suicide, there is no reason for her to come to Paris. She had as many opportunities to do it in Lausanne as here."

"She doesn't want anyone to find her, to find her body."

"And how is she going to do that? Bury herself? If she jumps in the Seine, her body will come to the surface one day or another."

"She might be unrecognizable."

"Besides, why would she come to see me? To tell me what she was going to do and make her identification easier? There's another thing. You understand, I'm speaking frankly to you. This story of not being found again, that's typical Odile. She knows she will be recognized and that everyone who knows her will go to her funeral."

He sighed.

"You're probably right."

"You know, she has always enjoyed complicating her life. Not long after she was fifteen, she started to tell the girls, one after the other, that she wasn't a virgin any more.

" 'How about you?' she would ask.

"And if we answered that we still were, she would look at us with both surprise and pity, as if we were ill.

" 'It wasn't one of the boys at school, but a man. I wouldn't want to go to bed with a school fellow.'

"For more than a month she kept after us with her lost virginity. Everyone knew about it, even the boys in the class, and they looked at her curiously.

"It was about that time that she began to get very friendly with two of the young teachers. I don't know if there was anything between them. I don't think so.

"She would go and have a fruit juice and a sandwich in the little restaurant near Béthusy where they used to have lunch, and eventually they all sat at the same table and she didn't mind smoking in front of them, in spite of the rule . . ."

"I know all about that, Emilienne."

"Then why are you asking me questions?"

"Because I am trying to find her. She has her faults, of course. That is no reason to let her make an irrevocable mistake."

"That is exactly what I'm trying to make you understand. She is playing a part. She has always played one part or another. When she learned that I was going to take a course in Decorative Art at Vevey, she wanted to do the same thing, although she had never touched a paintbrush in her life. Two months later she threw it all up. She had to catch an early train and work hard, with no smoking."

Everything Emilienne was saying was true. It really was his sister she was talking about, but she did it coldly, and the picture that emerged was basically unlike her. The two girls had nothing in common.

"Oh well. Thank you for seeing me."

"What are you going to do?"

"Go on looking."

"She doesn't know as many people as all that in Paris. How many times has she been here?"

"By herself, four or five times. Each time for several days. When we were children our parents brought us twice and showed us the sights."

"You're a nice boy, Bob. Best of luck."

When he left her he was overcome by a certain uneasiness. He had no illusions about his sister's character, but it had just been soiled for him, in a few minutes. The picture that had been painted for him was true in its main lines, but at the same time it was false, because it lacked a spark that one always felt Odile had, a certain thirst for life, for the ultimate.

He found it difficult to explain to himself what his own opinion of her was. Wasn't she worth much more than a girl like Emilienne? And than most of her friends, whom her parents held up to her as examples?

Something, some force within her, pushed her to the limits, without worrying about what anyone thought of her. It was still the guitarist who had understood her best.

He walked slowly in the direction of Rue de Seine and went into the Hôtel des Rapins on the off chance. The fat proprietress was busy in the kitchen.

"Has my friend come in?"

"Ten minutes ago. You're lucky. They were shooting on a quayside, near Corbeil, and he fell into the Seine. He's changing, if he has anything to change into."

"What floor?"

"Room 31, on the third floor."

They must have been the cheapest rooms, up there, for the stair carpet stopped on the second floor. He knocked at the door.

"Who is it?"

"Bob."

"Bob Pointet?"

"Yes."

"Just a minute. I'm getting into my pants."

He opened the door a moment later. His clothes were rolled in a ball on the floor and a pool of water had formed around them.

Standing in the middle of the room, which was not very big, Lucien Denge was pulling on jeans and a yellow polo shirt.

"It was that idiot of a sound engineer who knocked me into the water by moving backwards without any warning. I couldn't stay there, soaked to the skin. I had to take a taxi, because we didn't have a car available. It's a low-budget film, almost all exterior shots."

"Are you happy?"

"Apart from my forced bath, yes. I'm second assistant director now. That's a step up. Up until last month I was only a stage manager."

"Do you hope to become a director?"

"You bet I do!"

He was a small man, oddly built, whose feet turned out as he walked. He had an India-rubber face and a perpetual grin.

"Will you have dinner with me?"

"As long as we go Dutch."

"Right."

"What brings you here?"

"I'll tell you in a minute."

Lucien pulled on his socks and put on black cloth espadrilles.

"Come on. There's a nice *bistrot* just around the corner."

It was a real *bistrot* which could only have been patronized by regulars, because there was nothing to attract the eye. There was no Formica, the tables were still of wood, the counter tin, and the proprietor in shirt sleeves and a blue apron.

"Good evening, Monsieur Lucien. What are you having?"

"A Picon grenadine."

"And you, monsieur?"

"A glass of wine."

"Beaujolais? I can recommend it. My brother-in-law sends it to me from down there."

Bob went over to the slate on which the menu was written: *Moules marinières, blanquette de veau,* cheese, apple tart.

They took their glasses and sat down at one of the tables, and a tall girl in black with a white apron came out of the kitchen and went over to them.

"You're dining here with your friend, Monsieur Lucien?"

"Yes."

"Will you have the chef's special?"

"Do you eat mussels?" he asked Bob.

"Yes indeed."

"Yes, we'll have the special, Léontine."

"You know my name isn't Léontine."

"I think it suits you. Your parents should have called you Léontine."

He winked at Bob and gave the waitress a slap on the buttocks.

"Aren't you ashamed of yourself?"

"Not at all."

"What will your friend think?"

"That we are very good friends and that you see the joke."

As she moved off he murmured in a lower voice: "Well, what is it?"

"I don't suppose you have seen my sister?"

"When?"

"Yesterday, say, or day before yesterday in the evening."

"It's at least three years since I saw her the last time. Say, she must be a very pretty girl now. She was a bit thin then, and she didn't have any breasts."

"She does now."

"A funny girl. She should have gone into the movies."

"Why do you say that?"

"You know her better than I do, since you're her brother. But I have watched her for a long time. Suddenly she will decide to be a particular character and one would swear that she is not acting, that she becomes that character automatically. Besides, I believe she does. When she grows tired of the role, or people aren't pleased with it any more, she chooses another skin."

"That's just about true, what you're saying."

"That's why I spoke of movies. She would have the chance, each time, to be a different person."

He interrupted himself to speak to the waitress, who was bringing the mussels.

"A bottle of Beaujolais, Léontine. My friend says it's very good."

Then, to Bob:

"Is she in Paris?"

"She must be. That's what she said in her letter."

"She went off without any warning?"

"Yes. And she's threatening to disappear forever. I'm questioning the few people she knows in Paris, in the hope that she may have gone to see one of them."

"No luck?"

"Not so far. Tomorrow I shall go to the Bureau of Missing Persons."

"It's as serious as that?"

"You've just said so yourself. That she chooses a part and that she really becomes that person . . ."

"Poor Odile. Basically, she's a great girl. I would even say she's worth a good deal more than most of her friends."

Chapter **3**

If Odile had not yet put her plan into operation, she would surely not have stayed all day and all night within the four walls of a hotel room.

She must have gone out, more probably in the evening—and as late as possible—than in the morning or the afternoon.

She had no liking for the nightspots on Champs-Elysées. She found them pretentious. And Montmartre, for her, was only an enormous tourist trap.

In her eyes there was only the Left Bank, and Saint-Germain-des-Prés in particular.

For want of even the slightest clue, Bob undertook to make the rounds of the most talked-about places. He made his way into night-clubs full of smoke and deafening music where, in the half-dark couples had hardly room to move their feet.

"A table, monsieur?"

"No, thank you. I'll be leaving again in a moment."

He would stand at the bar and order anything that

came into his mind. First, he would take a close look at the guests, always in the hope of seeing his sister. Then, once more, he would take the photograph out of his pocket.

"Has she been here last night or the night before?"

The bartender, who was often the proprietor, would look at the picture, frowning, and shake his head.

"It doesn't ring a bell with me. But, you know, with so many people . . ."

"If she was here, she certainly stayed until closing time, and I suppose that by then you have fewer customers."

"Yes. They thin out as the night goes on. No, I am almost certain I have never seen her."

He had begun on Rue Saint-André-des-Arts. Then on to Rue Sainte-Geneviève, Rue Saint-Jacques, Rue de la Bûcherie. Once, during one of his stays in Paris, he had made the rounds of all the nightspots in the quarter.

Some had disappeared, while new ones had cropped up.

He would order a gin and tonic, take a sip, pull the photograph out of his pocket, and ask the obvious question. As the night grew later and later he found his idea less and less good, and he wanted to go to bed.

"Just one more!" he would promise himself. That would be the last.

Saying each time that this would be the last, he

went to more than twenty nightspots, each one more crowded and smoke-filled than the last.

On the way, he remembered what the guitarist had told him: that he had taken her to his hotel room on Rue Mouffetard, where she had been lying, naked, on the bed, listening to him play the guitar.

It had been on an earlier trip, but it must have remained a bright spot in his sister's memory. That was why Bob finally went to that district. The place he entered, still promising himself it would be the last, looked more like an ordinary *bistrot,* its walls not too clean, the guests mainly of the hippie type. A dark, greasy-haired woman sang among the tables, accompanied by a guitarist whose hair was as long as hers.

There was no trace of Odile. He almost left. Nevertheless, he went over to the bar, where the hefty, thickly mustached proprietor stood. His chest seemed to have been poured into the undershirt over which he wore no shirt.

"A rum, please."

He suddenly wanted to change his drink, and he had just caught sight of a bottle of rum straight in front of him.

"The singer isn't provided by the house, you know. Here the customers do their own entertaining. There are some who only come for that. If they're not too bad, I give them a drink."

He looked at Bob and asked:

"Are you a student?"

"Yes."

"I thought so. Not many students come here. Lots of young English kids. Scandinavians too. All more or less hippies, but nice."

"Have you seen this girl before?"

He held out the photograph without the slightest hope. The proprietor scarcely glanced at it.

"If you had been here last night, you would have seen her at the third table, where those two blacks are sitting now."

"Are you sure?"

"As sure as I see you."

"What was she drinking?"

"Gin and tonic."

It was Odile's favorite drink. She drank whisky only when there was no gin.

"What was she wearing?"

"Is this a test?"

"I'm trying to make sure it was really she. Was she alone?"

"She was alone when she came in, yes."

"What time was that?"

"About a quarter past midnight. A South American who must have had some Indian blood in him was playing a strange flute. You get all kinds here, and the evenings are never the same. When the musician had finished playing, I saw she had changed places and had sat down at his table."

"What was she wearing?"

"Dark brown slacks and a yellow pullover, with a suède jacket."

It was Odile's favorite outfit.

"Did she drink a lot?"

"Three or four glasses. The Indian didn't drink hard liquor."

"Did they leave together?"

"I don't think so. I didn't have any reason to watch them more closely than any of the others. In any case, I saw him alone at the table later. Is she your girl friend?"

"No. She's my sister."

"Is she a student too?"

"No."

"Have you both been in Paris long?"

"Three days. But we've been here before."

"Together?"

"No. At what time do you close?"

"When the place begins to empty. Usually between two and three in the morning."

"I'll stay, just in case."

He sat down in a corner. His head was spinning a little because, going from bar to bar, he had drunk more than he had realized.

"Could I have a very strong coffee?" he asked the waitress.

"I'll go to the kitchen to see if the precolator is still on."

She soon brought him a cup of coffee as thick as

soup. The woman who had been singing had left. A group of five tourists came in, looked at the customers around the tables, and beat a quick retreat. It was not picturesque enough for them.

So he had not been mistaken. Odile had gone out the night before, but she had not gone to see her guitarist. She had wanted to see something new. Had she made the rounds of a few nightspots, as he had?

Bob's eyes were growing bleary. Why did Odile not want anyone to find her body or, at least, be able to identify it? It was an absurd idea, and he could not guess how she expected to carry it out.

If she were to throw herself into the Seine . . . But she knew how to swim and it would be difficult for her to drown herself. She would either be caught up in the propeller of a motorboat, or else, after some days, her body would come to the surface.

She didn't have a gun. Or did she? He nearly called his father right away, but he, in his bedroom, would not hear the telephone ringing in the drawing room. There was a revolver in the house. It must have been there for years; Albert Pointet kept it in a drawer in his study, though there was no risk of his being attacked in broad daylight.

Bob wanted to know as soon as possible if the gun had disappeared. He would telephone at about six in the morning, when his father would be alone, drinking his big cup of coffee, before taking his walk.

Each time the door opened he had a surge of hope.

The guitarist was playing again, alone, as if for himself, his head a little on one side. Some people were listening to him. He didn't play badly.

He paid his bill, sighing, for the customers were thinning out. He was on the point of going back to his hotel on Rue Gay-Lussac but, on reflection, he went in the direction of the *boîte* where he had gone the previous evening.

Odile was not there. There were only five or six people around and the little orchestra was playing softly. The proprietor came over to shake his hand.

"You haven't found anything?"

"I know where she was last night."

The guitarist was not long in joining them.

"She hasn't been here?"

"No. Have you any news?"

"She is alive. At any rate, she was alive last night and she was in a *boîte* on Rue Mouffetard. It's called the Ace of Hearts."

"I know it. They're only amateur musicians, but it's quite a nice place. Did she leave alone?"

"The proprietor says she did."

"I've remembered something she said to me when she came to Paris the last time . . .

" 'There are some people who are satisfied with themselves. I envy them. I hate myself. As long as I can remember I have hated myself.' "

"Do you remember what she was drinking then?"

"Gin and tonic."

Bob was beginning to feel the effects of tiredness and his drinks. He went straight to bed after setting his alarm for six in the morning. He would telephone his father, who would be downstairs at that time, and then he would be free to go back to sleep.

Suddenly it was morning and the sun was rising in a slightly misty sky. Trucks were going by in the street. He had a terrible taste in his mouth and was not very pleased with himself.

He called Lausanne. The phone rang for a long time at the other end before someone picked up the receiver. It was his father.

"Who's that? Is that you, Bob? Have you found her?"

"No, but she was still very much alive night before last. It seems that she goes to little *boîtes* around Saint-Germain-des-Prés."

"Alone?"

"It looks like it. But that's not why I'm calling you. Can you tell me if you still have your revolver?"

"What revolver? Oh, yes! That old thing a friend gave me when I was about twenty. It must be in a drawer in my attic."

"Would you have a look?"

He had to wait for a long time. At last his father's voice, out of breath, said:

"I can't find it. And yet I'm sure I didn't put it anywhere else. I have just asked Mathilde if she hasn't seen it while she was cleaning. She doesn't know what has happened to it either. Do you think Odile has taken it?"

"I don't know. The bottle of sleeping pills has disappeared from the bathroom . . . The revolver has disappeared from your study . . ."

In fact, his sister wanted to die but didn't know how she would go about it. And that did not keep her from spending a part of the night in the district around Place Maubert.

"Have you made the rounds of the hotels?"

"No. There are too many. And I think she won't have picked one in the Latin Quarter, where she knows we go . . ."

"What are you going to do?"

"First of all, I'm going to the Bureau of Missing Persons."

"Don't forget that we are Swiss citizens."

"But she has disappeared in Paris."

"Can you prove that?"

"I shall try to, anyway. Have a good walk. I'll do all I can."

He went back to sleep until ten o'clock. He felt no better. He drank his coffee and ate his breakfast without taking any pleasure in it. A little after eleven o'clock, he was on Rue des Ursins. He followed the arrows painted on the walls of the corridor. In that way he reached Room 4 and entered the room before reading "Enter without knocking." There was a uniformed policeman behind a light-colored, almost new desk.

"Can I help you?"

"I'd like to see the director."

"There is no director. There is a chief superinten-dent. Do you want to inform us of a disappearance?"

"The case is quite complicated. I should like to see the chief superintendent in person."

The policeman pushed a pad toward him. The sheets were printed with several questions. He filled up the spaces in pencil, and the policeman disappeared down a corridor.

"The superintendent is engaged. He will see you when he is free."

"Do you think that will be long?"

"Your guess is as good as mine."

"Have I got five minutes, at least?"

"Certainly."

"I'll be right back."

He went down the stairs four at a time and went into the first bar he saw.

"A glass of white wine."

"Vouvray?"

"That'll do."

He needed to rinse his mouth. His coffee and his breakfast were sitting heavily on his stomach.

It was a small glass, and he drank it at one gulp.

"Give me another."

He very nearly ordered a third, but prudence stopped him. He already felt a little better. He paid, rushed out, and a minute later had taken his place again in the room where the uniformed policeman was.

"The superintendent hasn't called for me?"

"No . . . Wait a moment . . . That is his visitor leaving now."

He could hear voices in the distance, then steps in the long corridor.

"Will you come this way?"

The superintendent was a broad-shouldered man smoking a very black cigar.

"Take a seat."

He himself sat down at his desk.

"Who has disappeared?"

"My sister."

"Is she a minor?"

"She has just had her eighteenth birthday."

"Has she ever run away before?"

"No."

"Why is it you who have come? Are your parents no longer alive?"

"Yes, they are. But my father doesn't leave home any more if he can help it."

"You have put down the address of a hotel on this slip of paper. I suppose that is not your home address. Where is your home?"

"In Lausanne."

"You are Swiss? Are you studying in Paris?"

"No. I am a student in Switzerland."

"And your sister?"

"She has been here for four days . . . No, three . . .

I really don't know any more. There's been so much . . ."

"Actually, your case is none of our business. Even if you lived in France, outside Paris, you would have to go to the Prefecture, which would in turn consult us. Besides, your sister has only just disappeared. Have you any proof that she is in Paris?"

"Yes. I picked up the scent last night in a nightspot on Rue Mouffetard. The proprietor recognized her photograph. He also gave me an exact description of her clothing."

"Give me that description."

"Dark brown slacks, a yellow pullover, and a suède jacket like mine."

"What was the name of the *boîte?*"

"The Ace of Hearts."

"I know it. Couldn't she be staying with relatives or friends?"

"I have seen the few friends we have in Paris."

"There might be some you don't know about."

"I've met one already, a guitarist in Saint-Germain-des-Prés, with whom she went out on her last trip."

"So she has been here before?"

"Yes, with my parents' permission."

He took the photograph out of his pocket and held it out to the superintendent, who looked at it carefully.

"What kind of girl is she?"

"Rather odd. She dropped out of school before the last year . . . Then she tried various things . . ."

69

"And men?"

"Yes. She had her first experience shortly after she was fifteen."

"Still with your parents' permission?"

"No. I was the only one she confided in. Right from the start she was disappointed with sex, but she went on, anyway."

"Did she have any girl friends in Lausanne?"

"When she was at school I knew them. Afterwards she became more independent. She would often go out in the evenings and come in at one or two in the morning."

"Did your parents accept this situation?"

"It wouldn't have helped to argue with her. She would still only have done what she wanted to."

The superintendent chewed on his cigar without hiding his surprise.

"What does your father do?"

"He writes history books. You must have seen some in bookshop windows, because his publishers are in Paris and his books are very popular. He writes under his own name: Albert Pointet. He could have taught at the University of Lausanne, because he has his teaching certificate."

"If I understand you rightly, he is not very interested in you or in your sister."

"I think he has given up on us."

"And your mother?"

"My mother sleeps and plays bridge."

"Does she drink?"

Why did he ask that question?

"Two or three whiskies toward the end of the afternoon."

"So in fact your sister enjoys perfect liberty . . . Why did she come to Paris?"

"Because for her Paris is the only place that matters. Not just Paris. It's Saint-Germain-des-Prés that fascinated her."

He was annoyed with himself, in a superstitious way, for having used the past tense, and he corrected himself:

". . . that fascinates her."

"I don't see, under the circumstances, what my men can do. Even if we find her we can't take her back by force to Lausanne, where your parents are not going to chain her up."

"Read this letter. She mailed it, probably at the station just before she caught the train, and I received it the next morning."

The superintendent read the letter very carefully.

"I see why you would be worried," he said at last, pushing it back to Bob. "Leave me the photograph anyway. I'll have a number of copies made and pass them around to our men."

"You don't think it will be too late?"

"We shall do all we can, Monsieur Pointet. But you must admit your sister is not a predictable person."

"That is true. May I have the photograph back this evening? I need it to show to people."

"Come back around five o'clock. The man on duty

will give it back to you and he will also give you two or three additional copies."

He stood up, drew on his cigar, and shook Bob vigorously by the hand.

He had stayed in the district, having his lunch in a small neighborhood restaurant that he found without any difficulty, since they can be found almost everywhere in Paris.

Seated alone at a table, he watched the people passing by, but it was of Odile that he was thinking. Would she, too, be eating in a *bistrot* of the kind she liked?

Was it not more likely that, especially if she had gone to bed late, she would simply nibble a sandwich in bed as she so often did at home?

Not without an uneasy feeling, he wondered if she had already gone ahead with her project or if she had given herself a few more days' respite.

Was she still in the same state of mind as when she had written him the letter posted at the station? If not, if that had only been a transitory depression, would she not now regret having sent it to him?

All sorts of thoughts crowded in on his mind and he had the impression that he had done nothing since his arrival in Paris. And yet he had almost found her, at the Ace of Hearts. If he had gone there one evening earlier, he would have found himself face to face with his sister.

He had not tried all the restaurants. It was an almost impossible task for one man by himself. In the Latin Quarter alone there were hundreds. There were at least as many hotels to which she might have gone.

He toyed with the idea of asking the newspapers to publish her photograph. He could easily write a short paragraph that would move her. He had almost mentioned it to the superintendent in the morning, but at the last moment he had kept silent, believing that he might precipitate matters by doing that.

She was sensitive to the opinion of others. It was difficult to explain. She did all she could to shock those with whom she lived, but she remained attentive to the opinion they had of her.

She despised them, found them idiots and reactionary. At the same time she wanted to be loved, and that was why she was so generous.

When he left the restaurant he took a taxi and asked to be taken to the Forensic Institute, where an official in a waiting room asked him:

"Have you come to identify a body?"

"I don't know. My sister has disappeared, and I have exhausted the most likely places of finding her."

"Did she have any reason to commit suicide?"

"She said she would, in a letter."

"What name?"

"Odile Pointet. She wouldn't necessarily have her bag and her papers on her."

"That is what happens most often, in fact. How old is she?"

"Eighteen. She is blonde, quite tall, and thin. She was probably wearing brown slacks . . ."

"When did she disappear?"

"She was last seen night before last in the Rue Mouffetard area."

"In that case, she is not here. We have had three bodies in the last twenty-four hours, but none of them was a girl or a young woman. Leave me your address, just in case."

He had already begun to feel more cheerful when that sentence, spoken quite naturally, indifferently, chilled him.

He wrote his name and the address of the hotel on the Rue Gay-Lussac on a sheet of paper.

"Did you say that she told you she was going to commit suicide?"

"Yes. That was about four or five days ago."

"In that case there is little chance that she will. When one really wants to die one doesn't worry about other people and one does it right away. The moment one takes time to think . . ."

A little later he stopped at a kiosk and bought a map of Paris. The list of hospitals was on a blue page. There were fifty, some of them near the Latin Quarter, others more or less distant from it.

He went into the first one that was on his route. A middle-aged woman in a white uniform and cap sat in a glass cage in which there was a small opening.

"If you wish to visit someone . . ."

She pointed with the end of her pencil to the notice giving the days and hours when visiting was permitted.

"No. I am looking for someone."

"Someone you think may be here?"

"I don't know. It's a girl of eighteen."

"Has she had an accident?"

"Not as far as I know. She's my sister."

He was upset, and the severe expression of the woman did nothing to reassure him. He became muddled in his explanations.

"What I am afraid of is that she has tried to do away with herself."

"What makes you think that?"

"A letter she sent me, in which she spoke of committing suicide."

"What is her name?"

"Odile Pointet."

"What district does she live in?"

"She lives in Lausanne, but I know that she was in Paris night before last."

She consulted a list.

"There's no girl of that name here, and there hasn't been a suicide for a week."

"A week ago she was in Lausanne."

That was true. He could hardly believe it. Four days ago, Odile was still sharing family life at home. A life which suddenly, in the bustle of Paris, seemed so strange to him that it became unbelievable.

He had always taken for granted that things on

75

Avenue de Jaman were as they should be. His father had a rather idiosyncratic way of arranging his days, but was that not through lack of more contacts with his wife?

He never saw them together in the drawing room, not even in front of the television, which did not interest his mother.

She came to life particularly in the afternoon, to play bridge, and in the evenings she would go to the Nouveau Club, on Avenue de Rumine, to play bridge again.

He himself paid little attention to Odile. It was true that his studies were very demanding and left him little free time.

He went into another hospital, where his welcome was a little more friendly.

"A young girl, did you say? And recently? Just a moment, while I ask the head nurse if there have been any admissions in the last few hours."

She disappeared at the end of the corridor where a patient was waiting on a stretcher.

"No, young man. Nothing like that . . . I hope you get the same reply everywhere."

He finally found himself at the foot of Rue Saint-Jacques again, in the area where most of the hospitals are. He went to all of them, patiently. He repeated the same things. They received him well in some cases, badly in others. He didn't care.

"No, monsieur."

He virtually expected them to add: "Sorry."

He went by Rue Gay-Lussac to make sure that there had been no letter or message for him. For his sister would know that after receiving her letter he had taken the first train for Paris. And the family always stayed at the Hôtel Mercator.

"Nothing for me? No letters, no messages? No telephone call, either?"

"Nothing at all. Listen, you look exhausted. You would do better to go to bed early this evening."

He smiled with some bitterness. It was precisely in the evenings that he had a slight chance of running into Odile.

"I'll do my best," he promised.

At five o'clock he went to the Rue des Ursins, where he was given half a dozen photographs.

He couldn't take any more, and he went back to the hotel, where he stretched out on his bed. He fell asleep immediately, and when he woke night had fallen and his room was lit only by reflections from a streetlamp.

He showered and dressed. He thought he could hear thunder in the distance, but he was not sure. It was ten o'clock. He went into the first bar he came to and had three sandwiches and a glass of beer because he did not feel up to sitting in a restaurant.

Did the rolling of thunder sound like the noise of a train? In any case, he thought of a train, of his sister, her blue suitcase in hand, getting out on the platform.

If she had taken her suitcase, that meant she did not intend to commit suicide right away. She knew she would not stay on Rue Gay-Lussac, where the family would easily find her. She had never stayed at any other hotel in Paris.

Why not stay near the station? There were many hotels of all kinds. In the continual coming and going, she would be less noticed than anywhere else.

He took a taxi to the Gare de Lyon. Here he only had to say her name, as travelers were obliged to show some form of identification.

"Mademoiselle Pointet, please."

"Is she supposed to be staying here?"

"I don't know."

"We have no one of that name."

He went from one hotel to another. Each time they shook their heads.

Until one of the night porters said casually:

"You have just missed her."

"She was here?"

"Yes."

"When did she leave?"

"Yesterday, early in the afternoon. She took a taxi."

"Did you hear what address she gave?"

"I'm not here in the daytime."

He wanted to be sure that it was really Odile.

"Did you see her?"

"Certainly. When she came in at night it was always I who was on duty. A very nice girl, but not very happy."

"Was she wearing slacks?"

"Yes. She didn't change her clothes. She always wore the same brown slacks."

She had not gone to the station to catch a train, for she would not have taken a taxi. Why had she changed hotels?

"May I use the telephone?"

"A local call, in Paris?"

"Yes."

"You will find the phone booth on the left, in the hall. Wait, I'll give you a token."

He rang the Bureau of Missing Persons and asked to speak to the chief superintendent, whose name he did not know.

"You really want to speak to Monsieur Lebon? I'll see if he is free."

The slightly rough voice of the superintendent said:

"Who is speaking?"

"I came to see you this morning."

"Are you the Swiss who was looking for your sister? Have you found her?"

"No, but I have found the hotel where she spent her first three days. She checked out yesterday afternoon and went off in a cab. I'm sorry to disturb you at this hour. I am leading such a life that I don't realize what time it is any more."

"In the police force we don't keep set hours. You

are lucky that I had a report to finish and I came back to the office after dinner. What you have just told me is very interesting. That could actually serve as a starting point. What is the name of the hotel?"

"Just a minute. I didn't note it, but I can read it from here. It's an odd name: the Hôtel Héliard."

"Opposite the Gare de Lyon?"

"Yes."

"I know it. My men will see to that tomorrow."

"Thank you."

He was quite pleased with himself because he had had the idea of looking near the station. But why had Odile suddenly left a hotel where she had every reason to believe that no one would come to look for her? Was it too far away to reach late at night, when she l ft the Latin Quarter? Had she gone to some place near Saint-Germain-des-Prés?

He started his round in the basement bar with the big Scandinavian proprietor. He found the same musicians there, including the guitarist. He went to the bar and ordered a Scotch. When the music stopped, the guitarist came over and sat on the next stool.

"Have you seen her?"

He shook his head.

"But I heard a friend of mine, who eats in the same *bistrot* I do, speak of her. He's a guitarist too. He doesn't belong to a group and he gets what work he can. He is often at the Ace of Hearts, a nightspot on Rue . . ."

"I know. I went there night before last. My sister was there the night before. They noticed her because she isn't the usual type for that place. They were able to describe her to me exactly. What astonishes me is that, knowing you, she didn't come here again. Unless she is avoiding this place precisely because she is afraid to see you again.

"She is fairly sure that I am in Paris. She is running away from me. Perhaps she imagines that my father is here with me. I'll wait here a little, anyway."

When the music started again, he went over and sat in a corner where a beautiful girl who could not have been wearing anything under her black silk dress came over to him and said:

"Are you dancing, lover?"

"No, thanks."

"Will you buy me a drink?"

"Get one at the bar and put it on my bill."

"Don't you like my company?"

"It's not that, but . . ."

He stammered, taken by surprise, and she sat down calmly opposite him.

"Whisky?" the waitress asked her as if she had known her tastes for a long time.

"A double."

She seemed overcome by doubts.

"I hope you're not one of those?"

He shook his head.

"You're not from Paris?"

"I'm from Lausanne."

"That's in Switzerland, isn't it? I heard someone talking about Switzerland not very long ago . . . Yesterday or today, but I can't remember where it was."

"Was it a girl?"

"I don't know. I have the feeling it was a woman's voice."

"In a restaurant?"

"That's possible. I always eat at the Bilbouquet, on Place Maubert. But I don't think it was there."

"Do you live in a hotel?"

"No. I have a room of my own, where I can cook if I want to. I'm trying to think . . . Switzerland twice in two days, you must admit that's a strange coincidence . . ."

She was looking at him as she talked and seemed to find him agreeable.

"Are you in Paris for long?"

"I don't think so."

"Are you a student?"

"Yes."

"Here's to you."

On any other occasion he would certainly have gone to bed with her, because she seemed like a nice girl and her body was very attractive.

He signaled to the waitress.

"Are you going already?"

"Yes. I have to catch up on my sleep."

He paid. The girl sighed:

"Just my luck!"

He waved to the guitarist and went out. It was raining, a fine drizzle which the Parisians had been waiting for for a long time, since here, as in Switzerland, September had passed without a drop of rain.

On the off chance he went to the Ace of Hearts, where the proprietor gave him a glass of rum on the house. He did not want it, but he did not dare say so.

"She hasn't been in?"

"No."

There were three this evening, all with long hair, playing music as they moved about the room.

The glass of rum just about paralyzed him, and he had some difficulty getting back to Rue Gay-Lussac.

He slept until ten in the morning and woke once more with a horrible taste in his mouth.

Chapter 4

"Bob leaves the house before the mail comes. If the mailman gives the letter to Mathilde, she will take it up to my brother's room.

"If by chance she leaves it downstairs and if by an even greater chance my mother gets up early, she will recognize my handwriting and won't be able to resist her curiosity."

That was her state of mind in the train. Her thoughts were not dramatic, and she avoided thinking of the action she was going to take and of the manner in which she would disappear.

What would her brother think when he read the letter? Would he discuss it with her father? It was possible. The two of them got on quite well, and Bob often went up to the attic to talk.

Would he tell him about the suicide? Or only about the disappearance, a kind of running away, in fact?

There was every chance that Bob would come to Paris and that he would look for her, but among five million inhabitants there was little likelihood that he would find her.

Night fell, and she left the dining car to go back to her seat. A middle-aged man, holding a morocco leather brief case on his knees as if it were something precious, stared at her and, when she happened to turn her face toward him, would smile at her in what he thought was an attractive way.

It was on the station platform that her mind suddenly seemed to go blank. People were rushing about and many of them bumped into her as they went by. She stood there without moving in the gray light of the dirty lamps, and everything, even her journey, seemed unreal to her.

At a loss, she wondered what she had come for. She nearly got into a taxi to go to the Hôtel Mercator on Rue Gay-Lussac, where she would find herself in a familiar atmosphere. She could not go there. It was there that all the family had stayed for years and there that Bob would undoubtedly go first of all.

Opposite the station there was a row of hotels where only a few of the lights were kept on in the hall at night.

She went into the first one she came to, without looking at the name. The night porter, a sad-looking man, asked for some identification. She had not thought of that. It would be the same everywhere, and she took her passport out of her bag.

Her room was quite big, but ugly, a dull ugliness,

old, and of doubtful cleanliness. In the bathroom the water dripping from the faucets had left a long brown stain on the enamel.

Then, sitting on the bed, she began to cry. She felt alone, without anything to hang on to. No one had ever paid any attention to her and held out a hand to help her. Had anyone ever helped her to live?

It was stupid. Everything was stupid. Existence had no meaning, no purpose. She had been battering herself against the walls like a large fly on a hot summer's day.

She almost went out, to go anywhere, just to see the people walking, the cars, the lights. To escape from this emptiness which surrounded her.

Outside it would be the same. She would still be alone, and the passers-by could do nothing for her.

She took the bottle of sleeping pills from her toilet case and was tempted to swallow the entire contents.

Not yet. She wanted to give herself the time to live her death. She was still too lucid. She took only one tablet and swallowed it with a little water from the tooth glass. Then, lying on the bed, she cried a little more.

She did not dare to undress, as if she did not feel safe in that hostile room, and eventually she went to sleep fully dressed.

In the morning she found the same décor, which was no more attractive in daylight. It was almost midday. She did not feel up to taking a bath or a shower and going out. There was a telephone on the bedside table and she asked if she could have sandwiches brought up.

"What kind, mademoiselle?"

"Two ham and two cheese."

She ate them in front of the window, watching the taxis coming and going, taking passengers to the station or bearing them away.

She slept again and did not wake until four o'clock. She washed and dressed then, in a hurry to be out of doors, to escape from those four walls.

She walked along the Seine thinking mechanically of drowning. She could not drown herself. She was too good a swimmer and would instinctively stay afloat.

She had dinner in a small restaurant on Quai de la Tournelle. She did not yet feel a sense of reality. She had real dizzy spells. Her head was spinning. She wondered if she were ill. It was a thought she had often had, for several years.

"I shan't live to be old . . ."

She had said that to Bob two years ago, and Bob had laughed at her.

"Oh, that's just one of your ideas, my dear."

"Then why do I always have these sicknesses?"

"Everyone has, but they don't pay any attention to them."

She ended up in a little *boîte* on Rue Saint-André-des-Arts, watching the couples dancing.

They were happy. There were such things as happy

people. She drank gin and tonic, which added to her gloom.

She would have liked to talk to someone. To her brother, for example. No. Rather to a doctor, a specialist who would perhaps find the root of her illness.

But what illness was it? What had she done with her life until now? And it was no one's fault, not even that of the lugubrious atmosphere of the town.

She alone was responsible. She was unable to think of anything but herself, her ailments, the future which she was incapable of imagining.

She was useless. She gave nothing. On the contrary, she was a burden on others.

And now there was nothing beyond the present.

She had made a decision. She had written to Bob and tried to tell him everything. Bob was her opposite, a serious boy, stable, sure of himself. What had he thought when he understood her message?

At that very moment he was probably in the train, the same T.E.E. in which she had come to Paris.

She was tempted to allow him enough time to arrive, to go and see him on Rue Gay-Lussac, to tell him that she would give up her plan if he would promise not to tell their parents or anyone else where she was.

She would not go back to Lausanne. What would she do? She had left school too early to have a diploma that would be any use for anything. It was the same with her guitar lessons, her English lessons, her dancing lessons.

She would suddenly take off in a new direction, and for a couple of weeks she would feel a sort of euphoria. She would want to go more quickly than her teachers, who tried to calm her fever.

Then, from one day to the next, nothing mattered any more. She would leave a note for Mathilde before going to bed.

"Don't wake me tomorrow morning. Call up the English class and say I am ill."

Then she would isolate herself in her room and would only come down for dinner. She would sleep, play records, read whatever came to hand.

A middle-aged man sat down beside her.

"This is the first time you've come here, isn't it?" he eventually asked, leaning over her.

She looked at him as if she didn't see him, and he appeared embarrassed. She paid for her drinks and took a taxi back to the hotel. She did not have much money, hardly more than five hundred francs. What would she do when that was finished?

She was stupid. Had she not found the solution before she left Lausanne? She would disappear. She did not wonder any more what to do so that her body should not be found or identified. She had had that idea in Switzerland. It was too romantic. Besides, it was proving to be impracticable.

She would suffer the fate of all suicides. The police would be called in. Her body would be taken to the Forensic Institute for the autopsy.

Her parents would rush to the scene, would stay on

Rue Gay-Lussac, and would have the body taken back to Lausanne.

That was the part that upset her most. And yet, when it was all over, she would not feel anything any more. And would there be a short church service? There would, unfortunately, be articles in the papers, and her former friends, girls and boys, would be at the funeral, as well as the tradesmen and her mother's bridge partners.

She would be in a long varnished box where she would suffocate. It was stupid to think like that. She would not suffocate, of course. But was it certain that one did not feel anything any more?

She took another sleeping pill, as she had done the previous evening. She got up shortly after ten o'clock and, after eating breakfast, she washed and dressed.

She put on the same clothes as she had the day before. She usually wore slacks and close-fitting blouses, to make the most of her figure.

She was not pleased with her body. She had almost no breasts or hips. At home, she weighed herself two or three times a week, disappointed when she had not put on a few ounces.

She lunched in a restaurant, on a street whose name she did not notice, behind the Church of Saint-Germain-des-Prés. Things were not going as she had imagined. She had not thought that she would be alone, that she would have no one to talk to. She could not walk the streets indefinitely.

She went back to lie down and stayed in bed all afternoon.

She kept putting off the moment of performing the final act. Not from fear, but because she felt a need for this slow good-by to life.

It was a sort of preparation. No one among those she passed in the street or who spoke to her in the hotel would guess the thoughts that were running through her head.

She went out in the evening, of course. She just had sandwiches in a bar, for she was not hungry. Bob must have arrived. How would he set about it? Where would he start to look? He would certainly go to Le Cannibale, because she had once told him that she had gone there and that she had had a good time.

She had been in a state of euphoria then, and she remembered with nostalgia the guitarist who had taken her home with him. She would have liked to see him again, to talk to him, perhaps to tell him of her decision.

It was too dangerous. Bob would almost certainly go to Le Cannibale. Would he speak to the musician? Would he tell Bob what had passed between them?

What did it matter, actually? She was not ashamed of the life she had been living for several years now. The worst memory was that of Uncle Arthur, who did not seem to be embarrassed himself, since he still came to the house from time to time. He remained the same, pleased with himself and constantly cracking jokes.

"Well, gorgeous, how many hearts have you crushed by now?"

He was her mother's brother. He made quite a lot of money. He was constantly on the move, at the wheel of a flashy car, going from farm to farm selling agricultural machines. Almost everywhere they would give him a drink, which he never refused.

Odile had another relative in Paris, an aunt of her mother's, who had never married.

She must be over eighty, and she lived alone in an apartment on Rue Caulaincourt. She had worked for more than forty years in the same office on Rue du Sentier and she must have some savings in the bank, as well as a small pension.

Odile had seen her only once, when her mother had taken her along to Montmartre. Her apartment was sparkling clean, and they had to wear felt slippers so as not to mark the waxed floors.

What could she have told her aunt? And would she not have informed her parents immediately?

It was funny to think of her, a stranger actually, at this moment. If she didn't go through with it, would she not become like her aunt?

She looked for a place where she could spend part of the night. It must not be too well known, for she was afraid of meeting Bob, who would be looking for her.

She ended up at the Ace of Hearts. A woman was singing. A guitarist accompanied her. When a girl with nails that were varnished but dirty asked her what she wanted to drink, she ordered a gin and tonic.

It was one of the two young teachers whom she used sometimes to meet in the *bistrot* who had given her the taste for gin.

She had imitated. She had always imitated someone. She had no thoughts of her own. She realized that. What was disturbing with her was that she understood herself very well but she was incapable of changing herself.

She looked at the lovers who were holding each other around the waist and kissing. The man had his hand on one of his companion's breasts, and it embarrassed neither of them that there were twenty or so people looking at them. Were they really looking at them? Wasn't everything permitted here?

At the table next to her were two men, quite young, with long hair and jeans.

"Are you waiting for someone, mademoiselle?"

"No."

"In that case would you like to join us?"

They were drinking beer. She went over to their table.

"What are you drinking?"

"Gin."

"Drink up so we can buy you another."

She did so, submissively.

"Are you French?"

"No."

She was beginning to smile faintly.

"Belgian?"

"Not that either."

"You speak French without any accent."

"I'm Swiss."

"From Geneva? I've been to Geneva twice, and once to Villars for the winter sports."

"My parents have a chalet at Villars, and when I was a child I went there every year."

"We might have met. Don't you go there any more?"

"My parents still do. I prefer the sun and I take my holidays on the Mediterranean."

"Are you a student?"

"Yes."

"In Paris?"

She had to be careful, for they might be students and they would recognize a lie right away.

"No. In Lausanne. I'm here for a few days only."

She had often lied in such a way. It was not to make herself seem more than she was, but because the truth was too complicated. One could not speak of holidays as far as she was concerned since she did nothing all year except take one class or another, for a brief period.

"Have you been here before? Do you know Old Mustaches?"

That was the proprietor, because he had enormous black mustaches.

"This is the first time I have been in this *boîte*."

"It's a bit of a gamble. Some evenings it's fantastic, and others it's flat. It depends on who comes. The guitarist isn't a professional. He comes here to play for his own pleasure. The singer too.

"Some evenings there are six or seven musicians. The proprietor knows what's what. He doesn't interfere. Even when half a dozen drunken Americans who threaten to break up the place come in.

"Do you know Paris well?"

"I've been here quite often."

"With your parents?"

"Only when I was small. I've been coming alone for quite a while."

"Always to the Left Bank?"

"Yes. This is where I feel at home. I have never set foot in the Louvre or any museum. I don't think I've been on Champs-Elysées more than once or twice."

"It's the same with us."

"Are you two students too?"

"My friend Martin is at Nanterre . . ."

She looked at him with some admiration.

"I'm taking my degree in English, and then I'll try to get my doctorate."

She had not expected to meet such serious boys in this *boîte*.

"Don't you have any girl friends?"

"Off and on, but nothing permanent. We prefer change. We take and leave as opportunity offers."

"And when you invited me to your table you thought I was one of those opportunities."

They both laughed. The student from Nanterre was not particularly attractive, but the other had a frank, infectious laugh.

"Do you speak English?"

"No. I studied it for six months and the results were terrible. Like everything I do."

"What do you mean?"

"That everything I try fails miserably."

She was surprised to find herself smiling too.

"What faculty are you in?"

"Arts."

"Do you want to be a teacher?"

"No."

"A literary critic? A novelist?"

She was quite surprised to hear herself laughing. But was she not the center of attention of the two young men? They were paying attention to her. They thought she was interesting. She was acting, and she hardly noticed that she was lying.

"Have you any brothers or sisters?"

"Only one brother."

"Older than you?"

"He's four years older."

"Is he at the university too?"

"Yes. He works hard."

"What faculty?"

"Sociology."

"Like me," said the student from Nanterre. "What year is he in?"

"Third year. Then he goes on for his Ph.D."

"I'm preparing mine now."

It was a commonplace conversation, and it was comforting. She was not thinking of herself any more, or of her plans. They chatted casually, with a reassuring lightness.

"Would you like to dance?" the boy sitting next to her asked.

"Yes."

There was very little room between the tables, and it only took three couples to fill the free space.

"Are you in any hurry to get home?" asked the student in a low voice.

"No. There's no one waiting for me."

"When I get rid of my friend we could go for a walk together, through the night. Do you like walking?"

"I do."

It was not true. She walked only when there was nothing else she could do. In Lausanne she would take her motorbike just to go down to Rue de Bourg, five hundred yards from home.

He pressed her fingers as if they were already two conspirators.

"Then we could go and have a last drink at my place."

She said nothing. Neither yes nor no.

"I'll tell you in a little while."

She had not envisioned that when she left the Hôtel Héliard. They sat down again and ordered more drinks.

There was a silence. The student, now, was a little embarrassed about the proposition he had just made. But it was two in the morning, and wasn't she alone in a *boîte* of doubtful reputation? What did she want, if not an affair?

He pressed his knee lightly against hers and she did not draw away.

"Do you see those two hippies opposite us? They are smoking marijuana."

"What if the police come in?"

"The police know about it. As long as there's no trouble and there's no LSD, they prefer to keep their eyes shut. Except for pushers, of course."

"Have you tried it?"

"Yes. Twice."

"Did you like it?"

"No. It made me sleepy instead of exciting me."

"What about LSD?"

"I was as sick as a dog. You see, there are still some very ordinary young people around Place Maubert. Your health . . . My name is Martin. My friend's name is Louis, but we usually call him the Terror because of his fierce expression."

He gave her a questioning wink and looked at his watch. She blinked her eyes as a sign of agreement.

"Well, Louis, shall we go?"

"Right. It's your turn to pay."

Louis left them on his own initiative because he had a motorbike at the door. Odile remained alone, in the long, badly lit street, with the one called Martin.

They walked for a long time in silence, and they could hear the sound of their footsteps. Then something happened that made Odile tremble, something that she had not been expecting. Gently, hesitantly, her companion had slipped his hand under her arm, so that they were now walking along like lovers.

It was hardly anything, but she was moved by it. It gave a different color to their meeting. She did not remember a man ever having walked arm in arm with her.

"Do you live around here?" she asked, just to say something.

"Not far from here. On Rue du Bac. We mustn't make any noise on the stairs or going through the living room."

He laughed, and his laugh was very youthful.

"The house is an old mansion divided up into apartments. My landlady has a long lease for a wing on the third floor, and since it's too big for her alone she sublets two furnished rooms.

"She insists that her tenants obey two conditions. The first is not to cook in the rooms nor, in principle, to eat there. The second is not to bring in women."

"A condition that you don't fulfill very often, I should think."

"On the contrary. It's very rare that I take anyone home, and old Madame Boildieu has never caught me out. She must have been very rich, because the furniture is wonderful. The carpets too . . ."

There was a door in the hallway, and he had the key. They went up to the third floor silently, switching the light on again at the second.

He put his finger on his lips and took another key out of his pocket. All was darkness and silence. Only in the big living room was there a little light coming through the shutters.

He took her by the hand to guide her and they reached a corridor where he stopped in front of a door. He had only to turn the handle to open it, then he closed it again. The key was on the inside.

"Here we are!"

He put the light on and kissed her. It was all happening as if in a dream. The room was very big, high-ceilinged, and crimson silk curtains covered the windows.

The bed was turned down for the night.

"Don't be afraid," he whispered. "We can do anything we like from now on, except raise our voices."

"I'm not afraid."

If she had met a boy like Martin before, she would perhaps have fallen in love and things would have been different.

He kissed her tenderly, and she felt that he really did feel tender toward her. It was a little as if he realized that in spite of her self-assurance she was only a child.

"What would you like to drink? Brandy or wine? It's all I have here, and the wine isn't very good."

"Brandy, then."

While he went to get the bottle and the glasses from an old cabinet, she took her jacket off with a natural movement. The furniture was Louis XV and the wood was beautifully polished.

"Your health . . ."

"To both of us," he corrected. "I would like you to have a good memory of this evening. I don't know if I'll see you again, because you will undoubtedly be going back to Lausanne."

"I am going away, yes."

Speaking like that in hushed voices and having to strain their ears gave their meeting a somewhat mysterious, romantic character.

"It's a pity," he said, "that I didn't meet you sooner."

"I think I'm sorry about that too."

With gentle, easy movements he unbuttoned her blouse and took it off and then took off her bra and laid them on the chair.

"My hands aren't too cold?"

"No."

Of the affairs she had had, none had been like this.

He tried to take her slacks off, but that was more difficult.

"Leave it. I'll do it."

And she sat on the edge of the bed to free her legs. She felt no embarrassment, no shame. All she had on was a tiny pair of panties, and she took them off too.

"Aren't you going to undress?"

"There's too much light, isn't there?"

"The bedside lamp would be enough, wouldn't it?"

The lampshade was red and bathed the room in a rosy light.

He was the less at ease of the two. Odile was thinking:

"This is the last time, my girl."

He slid down beside her and caressed her.

"I'm too thin, don't you think?"

"You're slim and tall, but not thin."

"I should weigh ten pounds more."

"And where would you put them? You want to get heavier, while most women are torturing themselves so that they will lose weight."

When he caressed her more intimately, she closed her eyes, and soon he was on top of her, entering her slowly. For a moment she thought that for the first time she was really going to feel pleasure. There was a beginning, and she stayed as if suspended there, holding her breath, but the sensation disappeared.

She did not let him notice anything. She had opened her eyes and was looking at him. He looked so happy! Rarely had she seen such happiness on the face of a man.

"You don't need to take any precautions."

That had no more importance now. She would not have time to be pregnant.

She had been wrong to think of that. When she felt him come into her, tears rolled down her cheeks. Not violently. She was not sobbing. She only moaned a few times.

"Did I hurt you?"

"No. Don't pay any attention."

"It isn't the first time, is it?"

"No. I'm not reproaching you for anything. It's a personal matter. I'm a fool . . ."

The tears were still running down, very warm, and they had the same taste as the tears at Ouchy.

She had been eight years old at the time. One day her mother had scolded her severely because she had hidden in the drawing room while her mother and her friends were playing cards.

On being discovered, she had been shaken very hard.

"Go to your room and don't let me catch you hiding any more."

What she felt most was the sense of injustice. She had not thought of listening to what the grownups were saying. Or had that really been a little bit her intention?

"She hates me and I hate her too."

She spoke to herself.

"I'm going to rid them of my company and I shall be rid of theirs."

She tiptoed downstairs. She crossed the garden and went through the gate. She went down the street straight in front of her and shortly afterward crossed Mon Repos Park, which she knew very well. She had been there countless times to play, but she did not look around.

She continued the conversation with herself.

"How can grownups spend all their afternoons playing cards? She does nothing else. It would never enter her head to help Mathilde, who is old and has to do everything. Of course there is Olga, the cleaning woman, but she only comes four times a week, just for the morning . . . And she's very ill and doesn't know it."

She went on walking. She wanted to go very far from the house. She did not ask herself what would happen after that.

Was it a way of punishing her mother? Now she was walking through streets she did not know, and she was quite surprised to find that she was beside the lake and that she had got to Ouchy.

She sat down on a bench where she was alone. And it was then that tears sprang from her eyes, hot, salty tears, accompanied by very few sobs. She had no handkerchief to wipe them away. She was wearing the smock she wore at home.

"What's wrong, little girl?"

The lady must have been old. Almost all people were old to her, even her mother and father.

"Nothing, madame."

"Is anyone with you?"

"No."

"Do you live near here?"

"No."

"Do you know where you live?"

"On Avenue de Jaman."

"And you walked here?"

"Yes."

"Do your parents know you are here?"

"I didn't tell them I was going."

"Where do you want to go?"

"I don't know. Anywhere. My mother scolded me and shook me. I wanted to punish her."

"Come with me. I'll take you home."

She took her hand and led her to a taxi rank.

"What number on Avenue de Jaman?"

"The house is called Two Lindens, but there's only one."

It was her father who opened the door, because his wife had told him what had happened. She was searching all the streets in the area, and Mathilde was doing the same.

"Thank you, madame. I must admit I was very worried."

"Your daughter is a very intelligent, very nice girl."

She remembered not only the tears but the words that had been spoken. Her father had taken her in his arms, which he almost never did, and had kissed her. Her mother had been the first to come back.

"Is Odile back?"

"She's playing in her room. A charming old lady brought her home. You'd better not go up now, and don't say any more about it."

After all that time she still remembered her tears, and she cried as she had cried then, naked in the arms of a naked man whom she had known for only a few hours.

"Don't pay any attention to me."

And she said to herself again:

"It's the last time."

He went to the drawer of the dresser to look for a handkerchief to dry her tears and tossed it to her, joking:

"Here, blow your nose."

A little later he started again and she did not cry any more. She felt well. Her body was relaxed. She did not think of anything. She would have liked to stay in that bed until morning, with this big, kind boy.

He filled the glasses again with brandy.

"To our loves."

She sighed, knowing what those words meant for her.

"To our loves."

She had never loved. She would never love. She

had only just found, and then only by chance, arms in which she felt at ease. Wasn't it time for her to go now?

She went into the bathroom for a moment, then came back and dressed. Martin was almost ready.

"You don't have to take me back," she said.

"You're not going back alone. Where are you staying?"

"Not far from here. Just let me out of the apartment."

This time he took a little flashlight. Taking her hand to guide her, he crossed the living room, and when they reached the hall they saw a sort of ghost, a very thin woman in a nightgown who was watching them, her arms crossed over her chest.

Martin hastened to turn the flashlight on the front door, and the figure disappeared.

They hurried down the stairs. On the sidewalk, Martin pretended to laugh.

"I'm sorry. You're going to be chucked out because of me."

"Don't be sorry. I was beginning to get tired of that atmosphere, which is too plushy for my taste. Where shall I take you?"

"I've already told you: nowhere. I have to go back alone. It will let me think."

"Do you have a lot to think about?"

"Yes."

"Serious things?"

"Some of them."

"I suppose I'm not part of your worries?"

"I've just spent one of the happiest hours of my life."

"And yet you cried."

"Precisely."

He put his arms around her shoulders and kissed her for a long time, more gently than before.

"Shall I see you again?"

"I don't think so. It's time for me to go back to Lausanne. If I stay any longer I shall go to the Ace of Hearts from time to time and then we shall meet again."

"I'll drop by every evening."

He watched her go off and turn the corner of Boulevard Raspail. She walked with long strides, breathing deeply. It was her night. She did not know why she thought that, but it was like a theme song.

If she were to marry a man like Martin . . .

It was too late, much too late. And if she told him about all the affairs she had had, he would be discouraged. Perhaps he would gloss over her affairs. But later? Would reproaches not come then?

She suddenly wondered how she had begun. Most of her friends at school swore they had never had relations with men, apart from a few kisses and sometimes a furtive touch. She knew that two of them were lying, but they were the two girls in the class who mocked at everything.

One of them, Emilienne, must be living about

where she was at this minute. It was she who had studied Decorative Art at Vevey.

And because she was at Vevey, where she went by train every morning, Odile had gone there too. For several months they had been very close friends. Emilienne had told her about her affairs. She found it natural to have sexual relations with men.

Other people must have known about it. But no one held it against her. She stayed on good terms with her girl friends, except for Odile, whom she reproached for being uppish and disagreeable.

She was now in Paris, where she was taking a course in Art History. She would get married. She would have children. And all her affairs would be forgotten forever.

And then there was Elisabeth Ajoupa. She was dark, with large dark eyes and a lazy walk. She was already well developed, a woman really, at sixteen.

Odile envied her because of her breasts. They had become friends, and one Saturday afternoon they had gone to the movies together.

"Have you ever made love yet?" Elisabeth had asked her as a rather daring scene was shown on the screen.

"No. Have you?"

"Yes, I have. But don't tell anybody. I think my father would kill me if he found out. The first was a friend of the family, a married man with a very beautiful wife, much more beautiful than me. He rented a studio in Pully where we used to meet.

"After that I had others. Three of them."

She held up three fingers, as if that were important.

They had lost touch with each other. A year later Odile had received a wedding announcement from Beirut. Elisabeth Ajoupa was marrying a doctor with an almost unpronounceable name.

She had not noticed how far she had gone. Now she was walking beside the Seine, and the moon was reflected in it. She was not afraid. She did not think that anyone could want her handbag. Two policemen on bicycles turned around to look at her in astonishment, and one of them almost went back to warn her.

It had not occurred to her to take a taxi. She wanted to think, to think until it hurt. She smoked cigarette after cigarette. The two brandies, after the gins, had made her gait a little unsteady, and perhaps her mind too.

"I must, mustn't I?"

She was not fighting against it. She had made her decision. She had informed Bob about it. Perhaps he had told their father.

Oddly enough, at this distance her father was becoming a more sympathetic character. He made her think of a big dog whose size is frightening but who is really quite gentle.

There had been one when she was a little girl, a Saint Bernard who belonged to the people next door. He used to come into their garden, especially when she was playing there.

He must have realized that he looked fierce, because when he wanted to get close to her he would get down on his chest and crawl toward her. He had become her great friend, and she would run to the kitchen to get pieces of sugar or sweets for him.

It was Mathilde who would scold her, for she had an almost pathological fear of dogs.

"How can you play with that huge beast?"

"He isn't a beast. He's a dog."

"A dog who would eat you up in one mouthful."

"When I give him something to eat he takes it so delicately that I can't even feel his rough tongue."

Why did that memory come back to her? Oh, yes, because she had been thinking of her father. When had he started to hide himself in his attic, and why? She would never know. He was already installed there when she was born. Their grandfather lived in the house, and what was now the drawing room had been his study.

No one had the right to go in there without being invited. She particularly remembered his white, well-trimmed beard through which he ran his fingers mechanically.

For a long time she and her brother had had their meals in the kitchen. Then, when she was about six, she had been given the right, along with Bob, to eat in the dining room, on condition that they should not speak.

Now the grownups did not speak either, so that

meals passed in silence. Her grandfather paid no attention to them. She still did not know that he had never recovered from the death of his wife and that he had spent the last ten years of his life hoping for death.

One evening, there had been comings and goings on the staircase, and voices in the old man's room.

A car had stopped at the gate. Odile had not dared to open the door, and Bob was asleep. For at that time they slept in the same room.

The next morning she learned that her grandfather was dead. He had called for his son, had spoken to him for a long time in a low voice, and the end had come before the doctor arrived.

Chapter 5

She nearly telephoned her father without thinking that it was four in the morning and that she would be making him come down to the drawing room in his pajamas.

She did not even know what she would say to him. A week ago, she had hated him, considering him horribly selfish. Suddenly she saw him in another light, a man who was resigned to life, who had made himself a little world to suit his circumstances.

She wanted to hear his voice. What would she have talked to him about? Two Lindens seemed less gloomy to her from this distance, as did the life she had led there.

She had always thought of herself. She never thought that she might be disturbing other people, finding it natural that they should put themselves at her disposal, even for a passing fancy.

Wasn't that the reason why she had lost her friends? Afterwards she would hate herself for it, would beg forgiveness. She was sincere. She would see herself with a cruel sincerity, but a week later she would begin again.

If she did not call her father after all, it was not out of consideration for his sleep, or to avoid upsetting him, but because at the last moment she found nothing to say.

A moment ago, while she was walking by the Seine, she had been full of ideas that seemed good to her. At that moment she needed to exteriorize herself, and she would have confided in the first person who came along. She needed a human contact.

She wanted to be listened to, understood, encouraged.

Now, in her ugly, badly lit room, she was empty. She had never felt so alone. Stretched out on her bed, fully dressed, she stared at the ceiling.

Why shouldn't she telephone Bob, who was almost certainly on Rue Gay-Lussac? He knew what was going on. He would be relieved to have news of her. She would hear his voice. She felt she needed to hear a familiar voice.

Then she pushed that idea away as quickly as it had come.

Everything would have been arranged for her if she had got ill, not here in her hotel room, from where she would obviously be taken to a hospital, but in Lausanne. They would call Doctor Vinet. He knew her well. It was in his office that she would unburden herself when she didn't feel all right with herself.

She did not know what illness she would have liked to have. Something that would frighten everyone else but which would not be likely to be fatal. Something also which would not disfigure her or leave her crippled.

That was an idea which came from way back. She couldn't have been more than ten years old when she had thought from time to time of what she called "a good illness."

She had had one, when she was five. Her parents, Mathilde, and Bob took turns being at her bedside. She had a fever, which distorted her vision and thoughts. The room around her seemed misty and people's faced were blurred.

Doctor Vinet came to see her twice a day.

"It's too late to isolate her. You have all been in contact with her."

The doctor was very fond of her. Even now, he was the only one to look at her indulgently, and even with a sort of complicity. When she needed someone to pay attention to her she would telephone him.

"This is Odile."

"How are you?"

He had known her since she was a baby and he still called her *tu*.

"Not very well. I would like to see you."

He was very busy. He hardly ever had a full night's sleep. And yet he always managed to give her an appointment.

As soon as she was in his office she felt better.

"I don't feel well, Doctor. I'm sure there's something very wrong."

Didn't she end up by believing it?

"What are your symptoms?"

"You don't believe me, do you?"

For the doctor's eyes were sparkling with malice, but an affectionate malice.

"I'll tell you that when I've examined you. What's wrong with you?"

"First of all, I feel so tired I can hardly climb the stairs. I tremble all over. Look at my hands. And finally, I have a perpetual headache. It couldn't be a tumor?"

"No."

He examined her carefully.

"Well, my girl, I may perhaps be disappointing you, but there's nothing at all wrong with you. You think too much about yourself. You spend your time wondering what could be wrong.

"Do you know what's wrong with you? You're using illness to try to escape from reality."

She knew that he was right, but she did not like him to say so.

"You sound like Bob."

"How many cigarettes a day do you smoke?"

"Two packs."

"You realize that that's enough to make you tremble?"

"I can't do without them. And neither can you. I've often heard you tell my father you'd given up smoking, and a few days later I would see you with a cigarette in your mouth."

"I'm not eighteen any more, my child."

To be ill forever. To have everyone standing anxiously around her, just as when she had scarlet fever.

She stretched out her arm to the bedside table and took a sleeping pill. Out of habit, for she would have slept without it. She had taken the whole bottle from her parents' medicine chest, for she had thought at the time that she might kill herself that way.

She wasn't so sure of that now. She had read an article on suicide in the paper or a magazine. It was about barbiturates and other medicines. Apparently too strong a dose, contrary to popular opinion, rarely produced death because it brought on vomiting.

She didn't know the right dose. She did not want to be found in a bed full of vomit.

It was for a similar reason that she did not like the idea of using her father's revolver. To make sure of success, she would have to shoot herself in the head, at the risk of having half her face shattered.

She did not want to die here, in this room which she detested. Why did she not go on thinking about the delightful evening she had had? For once luck had been with her.

The young man, who had been a stranger to her just a short time ago, had been very attentive and very tender. She remembered the moment when he had put his arm under hers quite naturally.

And that climb in silence up the darkened staircase.

And the ghostly figure of the old woman who appeared before them as she was leaving.

It was all good. It was life. Unhappily, that didn't happen even once a year, and there were all the other days, all the other nights to spend.

She slept at last. She did not get up to undress herself. She jumped when someone knocked at the door. She looked at her watch and saw that it was past noon.

She was just going to open the door when the chambermaid slipped a passkey in the lock.

"Ah! I see you're up. I'm sorry I knocked, but I thought you had gone out."

It was not true. It upset her work schedule if a guest stayed in bed until the middle of the afternoon.

"I'll be out in half an hour."

She wanted to leave immediately. She was suffocating in that room. She took a shower, flung her things helter-skelter into the blue suitcase and into the toilet case.

"Are you leaving?"

"Yes."

And she deliberately did not leave a tip. On the ground floor, she went to the desk.

"May I have my bill, please?"

"Are you leaving?"

"Yes."

"Are you going back to Lausanne already?"

"Yes."

She paid. If she were to take a taxi in front of the

hotel, they would know she was not going by train. That was why she walked across the street, went into the station, and came out again by another door.

The taxi driver turned questioningly toward her.

"Where do you want to go?"

She did not know. It was important, because it would be the place where she would spend the last hours of her life.

"Take me to Place Saint-Michel."

She felt a little lost there, with her suitcase and her toilet case. But she was on the Left Bank, where she felt more or less at home.

She went down a street on the left, a street she did not know, Rue de la Harpe, and she walked along the sidewalk for some time, looking at the signs.

Finally she found herself in front of a hotel that had just been repainted. There was a big green plant on either side of the door.

The interior, paneled in a light-colored wood, smelled strongly of polish. The woman behind the desk was young and pretty, and there was a baby crawling about on the linoleum floor.

"Have you got a room that's vacant?"

"For how long?"

"I don't know."

"We don't as a rule like to rent a room for one night only. Almost all our people are weekly or monthly. There are some who have lived here for several years."

"I shall certainly stay for several days."

"Can you show me some identification?"

She liked the place.

The woman took a key from the board and picked up the child and put it under her arm.

"Excuse me, but at this time of day I haven't anyone to look after him."

They stopped on the second floor. There was no elevator. The carpet was new. The room, which was very bright, had also been repainted.

"We don't have main meals, but we serve breakfast."

"Thank you. That will do very well."

She opened her suitcase and put the contents into the cupboard and drawers. She put the bottles from her toilet case on the shelf in the bathroom.

She looked around her, discomfited. She very nearly asked herself what she was doing there.

It was a nice place. It was clean. It was sparkling.

She was hungry and she went downstairs and found a little restaurant with checked tablecloths a little farther down the street.

Her last meal? Probably. And yet she felt nothing. It was in the arms of the young student that she had cried. Now her eyes were dry. She watched the bustle in the street through the window. It would be the same the next day and all the other days. The life of Paris would go on in the same rhythm. And so would that of Lausanne. And her father would take his constitutional every morning in Mon Repos Park and then go up to work in his attic. Her mother would play bridge with her friends. They would mourn her at first. Then they would not think of her any more.

She was of no use to anybody. And nobody was really concerned with her.

"Yes, the calf's head vinaigrette, please. And then the lamb chops."

Here too the décor was pleasant. A little artificial, the counterfeit of an old inn, but still very pleasant. Why shouldn't she have a gin?

All that no longer mattered. She could do anything she wanted. In an hour or two, in any case before nightfall, it would all be over.

"Waiter! A gin and tonic, please."

She drank two. She was no longer afraid. She felt calmer and more lucid than usual.

What she had always lacked, and what she still lacked, was someone to pay attention to her. Someone who knew all her faults, who would protect her from herself, who would tell her what to do or what not to do.

Something like a Doctor Vinet for her own exclusive use.

No such thing existed, obviously.

Her mother had played this role until she was about three. Then it was Mathilde who had taken care of her.

Bob was very fond of her. She was fond of him too,

but he had his own life and they saw each other relatively little except at mealtimes.

Would Martin, her young man of the previous evening . . . ? In his arms she had felt at ease. Contact had been established. But would it be like that if it happened every day?

If fact she was looking for something that did not exist—someone, rather, who would sacrifice his personality and his private life for her. It would need to be someone very gentle, very reassuring, someone too with whom she would not get bored.

She smiled ironically. Without moving her lips, she was carrying on a conversation with herself.

"That's you all over again, my girl! Just when you are going to give up life, you start dreaming of what has never existed."

It was a sunny day. There were two tables out on the terrace, but no one was sitting at them.

"Like this? A little more?"

The waiter who served her had an Italian accent, and he was quite handsome.

"Just a little more, thank you."

She ate heartily, while at home they accused her of merely picking at her food.

Where would Bob be just then? Probably having lunch, too, in a little restaurant. He was a well-balanced person. He would be a good husband, capable of understanding his wife and children.

What did he think of her? He had always had, in

spite of himself, a slightly protective manner, a little as if he considered her to be an invalid.

Was she mentally ill? She had often thought about that. It was one of the reasons why she asked to see Doctor Vinet so often.

And Vinet, too, had astonishing patience with her. Wasn't it because he knew it was not her fault that she was as she was?

The lunch was good. She had ordered a red wine. She looked vaguely at two men opposite her who were discussing real estate. Wasn't it odd that so many people worried about so many things that had no importance at all?

"For dessert, mademoiselle?"

"What do you have?"

"Plum tart. I can recommend it."

She ate the tart, then lit a cigarette, refusing the coffee which would increase her trembling.

And that was that. She was on the street. She had nothing more to do. People were coming and going, taxis, trucks. They were all rushing to a destination they considered important. What importance had she not given in the past to her weekly marks? She did not even know any more what had become of her old notebooks.

It was after two o'clock, and the shops were open again. She went into a drugstore.

"A packet of razor blades, please."

"Any special brand?"

"No."

She wanted to laugh. Did the druggist imagine that she was going to shave the hair under her arms, and perhaps her pubic hair?

She must not go too far in the direction she was going, or she would come to Rue Gay-Lussac.

She walked slowly. She was annoyed with herself for being so indecisive. It was not because she was afraid. She was not hanging on to life.

On the contrary, the idea of leaving it soon gave her a sort of lightness of spirit that she had never known before. She had no more need to carry the burden of her small body around with her, or to worry about her future. One could do nothing more for her or against her.

She looked in the shop windows, surprised at what was displayed there, as if she had never looked in shop windows before. A druggist in a long gray smock was piling plastic pails on the sidewalk near the open door. Two women were waiting, motionless and silent, in a hairdresser's shop.

It was a long time since she had had her hair set, or even washed. She was almost tempted. She would have liked at least once in her life to be beautiful.

She went in and spoke to the girl at the counter.

"When can I have an appointment with the hairdresser?"

She could hear him working on the other side of the flowered curtain.

"I'm afraid he isn't free today. These women are waiting, and at four o'clock he has an appointment and another at five."

"Thank you."

Too bad! She wasn't going to go all around the district to find a hairdresser who was free.

Her legs were tired. She had walked a lot the previous evening.

She turned around and went back to her hotel, which was called prosaically Hôtel Moderne. She smiled at the young woman at the desk. The baby was no longer there. He would probably be sleeping in another room.

"Would you like your key?"

"Yes, please."

"Have you had a good lunch?"

"Very good."

"At Mario's, I suppose."

"I didn't see the sign. It's about a hundred yards from here."

"That's Mario's. It's very clean and the food is excellent."

People spoke just for the sake of speaking. When you got down to it they were perhaps afraid of silence. Wasn't it that which made her so ill at ease in the house on Avenue de Jaman?

Her father was hardly ever heard. Even when you knew he was upstairs you did not notice his presence. Her mother spent part of the day in her room and the rest with her friends, either in the drawing room or at the house of one of them, or at the Nouveau Club.

There was only Bob who could be heard coming up the stairs four at a time when he came back from his classes.

She went upstairs slowly, stopping on the first landing to look around.

It was the end. She could not go back. There was a touch of melancholy on her face.

If only she had been stronger . . . ? Strong enough to try once more? But she had tried so many times.

She turned the key in the lock. A ray of sunlight ran across the room.

Would it not be easier if she waited until night? She was thinking too much for that. She did not want to think any more. She was tired of it.

She shut the window, which the maid had left open, and the breeze from outside stopped puffing out the curtains.

She brushed her teeth automatically. Then, slowly, she undressed and ran the water in the tub.

As she looked at herself in the mirror, she suddenly felt again the need to talk to someone for the last time.

She only knew the first name, Martin, of the young man of the previous evening, and he had not thought to give her his telephone number.

When the tub was full and the faucets were turned off, she went into the bedroom, where there was a writing pad on the table. There were three sheets of paper in it and three envelopes with the name of the hotel. She had to hunt around in her bag for quite a time to find a ballpoint pen with a chewed end.

She was sitting naked on her chair. At home, in her own room, she often sat like that.

She nibbled the end of the pen for a minute before writing:

"Dear Bob,
"This time it's final. When you get this letter I shall be dead. I hope someone in the hotel will be good enough to stick a stamp on it and mail it. I have taken my clothes off and I haven't the strength of mind to get dressed again and go down.

"I can't remember any more what I told you in my last letter, which was written in the emotion of my departure. Now I am not nervous, and I find that it is easy to die. If I have allowed myself four days—I haven't counted them because the time has gone by so quickly—it is because I wanted to give myself a sort of respite. I don't regret it.

"I have been thinking a lot in these last few days and I'm not angry with anyone any more. I think I have learned a lot. I don't see people and things in the same way any more.

"I had a tendency to blame my perpetual depression on the atmosphere pervading the house. I still think it's not very cheerful, but Daddy and Mother can't help that. I am sure other houses are much gloomier and the children are happy.

"Besides, the proof is that you've become the strong man you are.

"Do you know, I've often envied you? And even hated you for your strength of character! Your look always made me a little afraid, because I expected to read irony or pity in it.

"I know now that was wrong. It's like my attitude toward Daddy, whom I no longer find ridiculous. He does lead a monotonous life, but no more so than men who go to the office and return at fixed times.

"Even Mother, who has found an inoffensive passion in life . . .

"In all this rather sordid story there's only one person to blame. Me. I've sometimes thought that before, but then I would soon see myself in a favorable light.

"Incidentally, while I remember, give my guitar, since you don't play, to someone who can't afford one. Give away my skis and skates too. I'll count on you to do that.

"I don't want anyone to keep anything in the house that belongs to me. I don't like souvenirs. It's a good thing I haven't had too many photographs taken. Well, there's another instance of my getting upset by the wrong things. At Emilienne's house there were lots of photographs of her, in every conceivable pose. Her father took them.

"I told myself that Emilienne was beautiful and

that was why they took so many pictures of her. I know I'm not beautiful, and there was no one, not even you, to take my photograph.

"I have spent four days reflecting on myself, to the point where my head started to spin. I'm not a dreamer, you know. I'm not a romantic either. I have, rather, a tendency to look at things and people coldly.

"I think I've discovered the chink in my armor. It's my difficulty in establishing contact with people. Did I tell you that in my letter from Lausanne? Perhaps I did. In that case, I'm sorry.

"At school there were groups of people, as there were in your time. I would be asked to join one of them. I was always made very welcome. For two or three weeks, perhaps longer, everything would be fine. They liked me and found me stimulating.

"Then, for no apparent reason, I felt myself different from my friends. They would look at me curiously then. There was always at least one who would say:

" 'Have we done something to annoy you?'

" 'No, why?'

" 'Because you're not the same any more. You hardly look at us. You go home right after school, and you always find an excuse not to go to anyone's house.'

"It is true. It is even true for the places where I find myself. I'll stop on the edge of the sidewalk and ask myself:

" 'What am I doing here?'

"It's at those moments that I feel dizzy. I have the

feeling that I'm whirling, on the point of falling. I'm tempted to stop a passer-by.

" 'Monsieur, could you take me back to my house? I don't feel well.'

"You know all that, and you have often said I was imagining things. Doctor Vinet did too, though he prescribed sedatives.

"If I am suffering from some illness, why does no one tell me? Perhaps that would take away the agony in which I live.

"Guess what! Here in Paris I have walked ten times more than I do in Lausanne and I haven't felt tired. At this moment I don't have a headache. I have no aches anywhere, and I could go on writing to you for hours.

"It seems I've still so many things to say. Soon I shall not be speaking any longer. Communication with people like myself will be cut forever. People like me? I hope for their sake that they are not like me. I am obviously not the only one of my kind, but we haven't met the others.

"Well, I must make up my mind to leave you. I believe it's of you I shall be thinking at the last minute. Think of me too from time to time, will you?

"I would like to be near you and have you hug me close to your chest, stroking my head absent-mindedly as you sometimes do.

"You can see I have good memories of you.

"I'm not going to read this over. Excuse the repetitions and the mistakes, if there are any. Excuse the cigarette burn too.

"If he mentions me, tell Doctor Vinet that I got up to three packs a day and that little by little I got a taste for gin.

"Ciao! A big hug. Good-by, Bob, dear brother.
                                "Your Odile"

She stopped for a moment and gazed into space, then she added, below her signature:

"P.S. As with my first letter, I must ask you not to show this to Daddy or Mother. I would like this to remain between us two and no one else to know anything about it. Thank you."

She wrote her brother's name on an envelope, with Hôtel Mercator, Rue Gay-Lussac, as the address. Then she added "Express."

She searched in her bag and brought out some change which she laid on top of the letter to pay for the postage. Then she thought about the rent.

"Dear Madame,
"Forgive me for the trouble I have caused you. The two hundred francs should serve to pay my rent and for the unpleasantness caused you.

"You have been very kind and I am very grateful to you."

She placed this note under the two bank notes and got up. She had finished. She walked over to the window through which she saw the street a little mistily because of the net curtains.

The street would be the same, with the same sounds, the same ordinary people on the sidewalk, tomorrow, the day after, and for years and years to come.

She lit a cigarette and with a firm step went into the bathroom and put her leg over the edge of the tub.

She had to get out again because she had left the razor blades on the shelf. She took one and sat in the water with her legs stretched out.

The cigarette smoke made her blink. She was not afraid. She was calm. She had promised herself she would take two or three sleeping pills just in case, but she had no need of them.

She looked for the vein in her wrist and made a long cut with the blade.

There was someone in the room, someone who was doing something to her arm and who smelled strongly of tobacco. She was surprised still to be alive, and at last she opened her eyes.

A tall, red-haired young man, his face and arms covered with freckles, was putting a tourniquet on her arm. The bath water, in which she was still sitting, was slightly pink, and that made her heart miss a beat.

"What are you doing here?"

"You can see. A tourniquet. Don't be afraid. It's a clean handkerchief which I got from my room. Yours were too small."

His skin had the same texture as an orange, and his eyes were a very pale blue.

"Why are you here?"

"Because you called out."

"I did?"

He had finished and he had also applied a temporary dressing.

"If you'd like to get out of the water . . . Have you a dressing gown?"

"There's one in my suitcase."

He saw a bathrobe that was hanging behind the door and held it out to her.

"Here. Put this on."

She could not read any thought in his expression.

"What do you mean, I called out?"

"You gave a sharp cry, and because there is just a partition between your room and mine, I realized it was a cry of anguish. I was afraid I would find the door locked, but it wasn't.

"You had fainted. I ran into my room to get a clean handkerchief and a toothbrush which would do instead of a stick for the tourniquet."

"I wanted to die."

"I did take in the fact that you hadn't slashed yourself like that just for fun."

"Is it deep?"

"Not very. When you saw the blood, your instinct was to stop and you cried out. Just once. Quite a scream."

"I don't remember a thing about it."

He helped her out of the tub and handed her the white bathrobe.

"I'm not quite a doctor, but I'm in the fourth year of my medical studies and I'm an assistant at Cochin Hospital. It's lucky that this afternoon I had some theoretical work to finish . . . How do you feel?"

"I'm stunned."

"I'll go and get a glass of something to set you up again."

He came back with a bottle of brandy and rinsed out the toothbrush glass.

"What about you?" she objected.

"I haven't cut my wrist."

"Are you going to make me another dressing?"

"I'm going to take you to the hospital where they'll take care of you much better than I could do here."

"Don't take me to the hospital, please. They'll realize it's an attempted suicide and they'll tell the police."

"Are you afraid of the police?"

"They'll tell my parents. And I don't want to go home, no matter what."

"Sit down. You can't be too steady on your feet."

"It's funny. I don't remember feeling any pain."

"You didn't feel any pain. It was anguish that made you cry out at the same time as you let go of the blade."

He seemed to hesitate.

"Do you live in Paris?"

"No. I'm from Lausanne."

"Do you have any relatives here?"

"Only an aunt of my mother's, whom I haven't seen

for at least ten years. I don't want to go home. If you
want to speak to someone who knows me, I can call
my brother, who is almost certainly staying in a hotel
on Rue Gay-Lussac."

"Is that letter addressed to him?"

"Yes."

"Did he come to Paris to look for you?"

"Yes. I had written to him and told him that I was
leaving home forever and that no one would hear any
more of me."

She smiled somewhat crookedly.

"It's funny!"

She looked at the place where she had been sitting
to write her letter, then she looked at her watch. Less
than twenty minutes had passed since she had sealed
the envelope.

"When can I see your brother?"

"As soon as he gets back to the hotel. You can call
now. You'll find out whether he is staying there."

"I have more urgent things to do. You must promise to stay here like a good girl and wait for me. I'm
going down to the pharmacist's to get what I need."

"You're not going to take me to the hospital?"

He looked embarrassed.

"You're lucky that I'm not a doctor yet, because if I
was, I'd have to inform the police about you. It's split-
ting hairs a bit. I hope you can keep your mouth shut."

"I promise you that."

She lit a cigarette with one hand, while he went

downstairs without putting his jacket on. He was tall, broad-shouldered and had rather thick features.

She did not remember crying out, but it came back to her now that she had had a sensation of falling and that she had tried to hang on to something, probably the edge of the tub.

Did the red-haired student believe her? Wouldn't he suspect her of having pretended to commit suicide knowing that she would call out at the last moment?

She had not known that he was there and that he was an assistant in a hospital. He had never seen her in the hotel, where she had arrived only that morning.

He came in, his arms full of small packages. Then he went into his room to get an alcohol lamp.

"Does it hurt?"

"A little. Hardly at all."

"I'm afraid I'm now going to hurt you a bit."

He disinfected his instruments by putting them in the flame of the lamp and he made five stitches.

Each time, she gave a start, clenching her teeth because she did not want to cry in front of him.

"Now I want to take the tourniquet off."

"Is that all?"

"For the moment, yes. Tomorrow I'll have to take the dressing off to see how the wound is."

His glance fell on the bottle of brandy.

"Would you like another?"

"I think it's doing me good."

He gave her some and sat on a chair turned backwards, one leg on each side and his arms leaning on the back.

"Are you pregnant?"

She started, more surprised than annoyed.

"Why do you ask that?"

"Because it's often because they're pregnant by a man they can't marry that girls try to commit suicide."

"That's not my problem. You said try. Are there many who are rescued?"

"A good half."

"If you hadn't been in . . ."

"I know. Call your brother now."

She asked for the Hôtel Mercator and recognized Monsieur Bedon's voice.

"This is the Hôtel Mercator."

"Is Bob Pointet staying with you?"

"He's staying here, but he went out about an hour ago."

"Do you know at what time I'd be likely to find him in?"

"A little before dinner, because he likes to take a shower at the end of the day."

"Thank you."

"May I give him a message?"

"Tell him that someone telephoned and will call back. He'll understand."

She put down the receiver.

"It's just as I thought. He won't come back till just before dinner to take a shower."

She took another cigarette, and he held out a match for her.

"May I?" he asked, taking a pipe from his pocket.

"Please do."

"How do you feel, being alive?"

"I'm more tempted to wonder how I would have felt being dead."

"A love affair gone wrong?"

"No. I'm not in love."

He looked as if he was thinking, then sighed.

"Have you ever done that before?"

"No."

"You've never been tempted to?"

"Often. Every time I have a period of depression, and I often have . . ."

"Who's your doctor?"

"The family doctor, Doctor Vinet."

"Have you talked to him about this urge to commit suicide?"

"I tell him everything."

"What treatment has he given you?"

"He tells me to give up smoking, to take a tranquilizer three times a day and two sleeping pills in the evening, because I can't sleep otherwise. It was the same when I was a child."

She felt at ease with this big, pleasant man in shirt sleeves on which there were a few little drops of blood.

He did not smile. He was not trying to appear amiable or otherwise. He was looking at her carefully as if he was looking for an answer to a question he was asking himself.

"Have you had a blood test recently?"

"Less than two months ago. We usually go, in our family, for a complete checkup and laboratory analysis every year."

"Are you still at school?"

"I should be at the *lycée*. We don't have quite the same school system as in France."

"I know. Why did you say 'I should be'?"

"Because I'm not. I left school without finishing. I have no diploma or certificate."

Someone was taking an interest in her, and it was a young man who seemed to understand the human heart. She had only just escaped death and she found herself quite whole again. She hoped he would ask her a lot of questions.

"Weren't you working just now?"

"Yes, I was working, but that can wait. May I ask your father's profession?"

"He's a writer. A historian, rather. He usually writes historical biographies."

"Albert Pointet?"

"You know him?"

"I've read three or four of his books. According to the papers, he writes one regularly every year."

"That's true."

The telephone rang. Odile hurried over to it, panicked, then she got hold of herself but had to make an effort to pick up the receiver.

"Hello," she said.

"So it's you!"

Bob was on the other end of the line.

Chapter 6

"Where are you?"

"Not far from the Hôtel Mercator."

"Are you all right?"

"Quite all right. I fouled it up, of course. Being me, I couldn't have done anything else."

She smiled at the student, who looked embarrassed.

"May I go to see you, or are you going to come and stay here?"

"I'd rather stay here, for the moment at any rate."

"Then I'll come. Where is it?"

"The Hôtel Moderne, on Rue de la Harpe."

"I'll be there in ten minutes."

The red-haired young man was still examining her with a curiosity that he did not try to hide. He was surprised by her, that was certain. He was trying to understand her. He could feel that there were undercurrents which were escaping him.

"I puzzle you, don't I?"

He didn't say yes or no. He watched her steadily, his face expressionless.

"I shouldn't think," he said as if to himself, "that, knowing what I know about your father, you had an unhappy childhood, did you?"

"No. But I don't have any happy memories, either. They often used to find me, silent and motionless, huddled in a corner of a hall or in the garage at the end of the garden."

"Why?"

"I don't know. Perhaps because I didn't feel comfortable with my mother, for example, or with anybody . . . I realized later that it was a little as if I didn't feel I belonged to the same race as the others."

"Didn't you ever play?"

"Very rarely. And when I did it was without much conviction."

"Can you remember now what you used to think about?"

"No. I don't think I thought at all. I would stare straight in front of me. I must have stayed for hours staring at a spot on the wallpaper."

"Didn't your parents get worried?"

"They thought it would pass. I would often hide myself in the house until I was found."

"Was it a way of getting them to pay attention to you?"

"It may have been."

"Did you have any childhood illnesses?"

"Scarlet fever. It's my happiest memory. I was in bed, with magazines. The maid would come up twenty times a day to make sure I didn't need anything. My mother's friends had stopped coming to play bridge because they were afraid they would catch it. My room had become the center of the household. My mother came to see me, too. My father would come down and sit by my bed."

"Generally speaking, did you lack affection?"

"I couldn't really say so. It was I who didn't understand. I had the impression that each person was interested only in his own private life and that I was more of a burden than anything else. May I get up? I want to go into the bathroom to dress."

The bathtub was full of pinkish water, and she pulled the plug. In her suitcase she found a pair of gray slacks and a paler gray sweater. Then she ran a comb through her hair. She heard voices in the next room and rushed through, knowing it was her brother.

"Oh, Bob!" she cried, burying her head against his chest, just as she had dreamed of doing.

"Dear little kitten."

He sometimes used to call her that, when he was being sentimental.

"Let me look at you. No, you don't look ill."

She felt happy, unconstrained. She had two men in her room when the odds were that she would have remained alone in the tub until the next morning.

"Let me introduce you."

She turned toward the student.

"I'm sorry, but I didn't even think to ask your name."

"Albert Galabar."

"My brother Bob."

"How do you do."

"How do you do."

Their manner was awkward. They seemed to be measuring each other up.

"If I've got it right, you came to Paris to look for your sister?"

"And I just barely missed her. First of all, in a night club where they told me they'd seen her the night before. Then this very afternoon, in a hotel she had just left, opposite the Gare de Lyon."

"You found the Hôtel Héliard?"

"I couldn't check all the hotels on the Left Bank. I guessed you would be afraid you might run into me. When you got to the station you rushed into the first hotel you came to, thinking no one would look for you there."

She shivered as she thought of her room.

"It was such an awful place."

"Weren't you afraid to stay so close to Rue Gay-Lussac?"

"I wasn't running any risk, because I'd decided to make an end of it today."

"What happened?"

He was holding her by the shoulders and he was so relieved to have found her that he looked more like a lover than a brother.

"I cut my wrist and it seems I called out. Albert

Galabar has the room next door. I didn't know that. I'd never seen him. When I opened my eyes I was still in the tub and he was putting on a tourniquet. He's a medical student, an assistant in a hospital."

The two men looked at each other again.

"It was by chance that I was in my room."

"Would the wound have been fatal?"

"Very probably."

"Is this letter for me?" asked Bob, pointing at the envelope on the table. "Why is there some change on top of it?"

"To pay for the stamp."

"And that money?"

"It's for the room."

They both looked at her in surprise.

"You thought of all that before cutting your wrist?"

"I was calm, not at all nervous. Before that I had gone to a restaurant a little way down the street, where I had a good lunch. After that I almost went and had my hair washed and set, but I would have had to wait too long."

"May I take the letter?"

"It's yours. Don't show it to anyone, especially not the family."

"Shouldn't you call Father?"

"I think I must."

She frowned. It was making contact with Avenue de Jaman, and it seemed to her she was going to be caught up in its meshes again.

"I shan't tell him I'm going to come back. I'll just speak to him."

He asked for the number. It was Mathilde who answered.

"It's Bob, Mathilde. I want to speak to my father. Mother isn't in the drawing room with her friends, is she?"

"No, she has gone out shopping."

"So much the better. Father will give her the news."

"You have good news, haven't you? I can tell that from your voice."

A few moments later his father was at the other end of the line.

"Is there any news, Bob?"

"Very good news. I've found Odile. Or rather she found me."

"How is she?"

"Very well, apart from a cut on her wrist. It's not serious and she has been well taken care of."

"When are you both coming home?"

"I'll probably come back tomorrow. I've already missed several important classes. I don't know about her . . ."

He signaled to his sister to come and take the telephone.

"I'll put her on."

"Hello, Daddy."

"What a way to scare us! When did it happen?"

"This afternoon."

"And you're up already?"

"Of course. I've never felt so well."

As she said that she threw a quick, conspiratorial glance at the student.

"Aren't you coming back with your brother?"

"I'm going to wait until I'm rested and my wound has started healing properly."

She could hear sadness, or at least a resigned melancholy, in her father's voice.

"I understand," he said. "Are you staying on Rue Gay-Lussac?"

"No. If you need to get in touch with me, I'm at the Hôtel Moderne, Rue de la Harpe."

"I hope you'll be home soon. You can't imagine how empty it feels."

"If I were to get married, it would be the same, wouldn't it?"

"You don't intend to come back for good?"

"No."

"Do you think you'll stay in Paris?"

"Yes. You know that's always been my dream."

There was silence. Someone on the line asked:

"Are you through?"

"No, mademoiselle. Don't cut us off, please."

"I'll come home next week to see you, then I'll go back to Paris to look for work. I haven't much to offer, I know. I don't have any diploma, but I hope I'll find something to do anyway. Have you seen Doctor Vinet?"

"I asked him to come around to see me. Why do you ask?"

"Because I was sure you would consult him. Not about you, but about me. You asked him what he thought about my running away, and if I would really commit suicide."

"That's right, I did."

"What did he say?"

"He wasn't very optimistic. I'll phone him right away and tell him the good news."

"Do that. Tell him I send him a kiss. A big kiss for you too, Daddy. I've been thinking about you a lot, and I love you more than ever."

"Thank you, my dear. Don't hang up. I can hear someone coming in. It must be your mother."

She heard voices away from the telephone and then her mother's voice, saying: "So, you're alive! Thank God! Tell me what's happened."

"Daddy will tell you, because I'm a bit tired now."

Besides which, she didn't know what to say to her mother.

"Are you coming home tomorrow?"

"No. I'll come and see you in a few days. Daddy will explain. And Bob, who is leaving tomorrow, will tell you both all the details."

The face of the doctor-to-be showed astonishment. She had just escaped from a voluntary death and she was already occupied in organizing the future.

She put down the receiver.

"Whew," she sighed, dropping into the only arm-chair in the room. "That's over with."

She appeared to have shed a burden and to be finding her feet again. She lit a cigarette.

"What did you say your name was?"

"Albert Galabar. My family comes from Toulouse."

"What I can't understand," murmured Bob, with a shiver as he thought of it, "is that you waited four days, almost five . . ."

"It was my holiday."

"What did you do?"

"Don't you know me well enough to guess? I went to night clubs every night."

"All by yourself?"

"I did that in Lausanne too."

"Did you drink a lot?"

"Not much. A few glasses of gin. That makes me thirsty for another drop of brandy. May I, Monsieur Galabar?"

"Of course, but call me Albert."

"Albert, then. I have a reputation for being too familiar rather than too formal."

She was not drunk, but she was getting light-headed. Was an event like that not worth celebrating? It seemed to her that she was definitely saved, that she had lost the worst part of herself.

"By the way, ask Daddy to send me some money, will you? I left home with about six hundred francs in my pocket. I changed them in the first hotel I stayed at, but I have almost nothing left."

"I'll give you a little now."

He took his wallet out of his pocket, counted the notes, and took out three.

"Will that hold you until you come home?"

"I think so. Since I'm going to keep the room, I won't have to pay for it right away."

"I'll leave you," said Galabar, getting up from his chair.

And, to Odile:

"I'll come and see you tomorrow. What time is the most convenient?"

"Well, you know, I'm a night bird."

"You'd better not tire yourself out too much today. Buy a thermometer at the pharmacy just down the street. Take your temperature when you come in, and don't hesitate to knock on my door if you're running a fever."

"Thank you. And thank you for everything you have done."

"Better thank Providence, which had me in my room this afternoon."

He shook her good hand.

"Don't drink too much either."

The two men shook hands.

"I may not have the chance to see you again before you leave. I'm very glad to have met you."

"And I to have met you."

When they were alone she threw her arms around his neck.

"It's so good, Bob."

"You can't know how afraid I was."

"Did you think I'd do it?"

"I know you, don't I?"

"I think you're the person who knows me best."

"Let me look at you again. You haven't changed at all. There's just a little light in your eyes."

"Don't tell anyone, but this time I think I've fallen in love."

"May I ask you with whom?"

"You've guessed already, haven't you?"

"Things move quickly with you. Is he the reason why you're going to stay in Paris?"

"No. But I couldn't stand the atmosphere of the house any more. Here! While I fix my face and hair, you read this letter. That'll save me having to tell you everything again. Although I can't remember any more what I wrote. I went out to buy razor blades. Oh! You can have the ones that are left. I had run the bath and I was already undressed and I started to write. I put down on paper everything that went through my head. I suppose it's stupid . . ."

It was such a short time ago that she had been sitting, naked, on that chair, writing with a ballpoint pen with a chewed end.

"You can't know how good it is . . ."

"I have a phone call to make."

"To whom?"

"You'll see."

He asked to be put through to the chief superintendent at the Bureau of Missing Persons.

"Do you wish to speak to Chief Superintendent Lebon?"

"Yes."

"I'll see if he is free."

A few minutes later a deep voice asked:

"Who is speaking, please?"

"I don't know if you remember me. I'm Bob Pointet, and I came to see you to inform you of my sister's disappearance. I have found her."

"Is she all right?"

"Yes."

"Where was she today?"

"In the Latin Quarter."

"What put you on her track?"

"She telephoned me."

"I'm happy for your sake, and for hers. I'll close the file, then. Good-by, Monsieur Pointet."

"Did you understand that?"

"I got the idea."

"There are thousands of hotels in Paris, hundreds on the Left Bank alone, where I thought at first you would come. Since I couldn't check them all, I went to the Bureau of Missing Persons."

"Shall we go out? I think the fresh air will do us good. Then we can both have dinner in the little restaurant where I had lunch. I was sure it was my last meal, and yet that didn't lessen my appetite. On the contrary! Read the letter quickly. I'll be right back."

She made herself up more carefully than usual, and brushed her hair, looking at herself in the mirror with satisfaction.

Why had she always thought she was ugly? She thought she was pretty today, and she noted her good points with pleasure.

When she went back into the bedroom, her brother was slipping the letter into his pocket. He seemed moved.

"There. You've read it. You have understood. Now we won't talk about it any more."

"All right, Odile."

His voice was a little hoarse.

"You're a funny girl, you know. I hope you meet someone who will understand you. It isn't easy."

"Come on."

She took her handbag and picked up the money on the table.

The baby was in his place on the floor again, in the office, and he was playing with bricks.

"Good evening, madame. This is my brother Bob."

"I'm sorry I don't have any vacancy."

"Oh, he's been staying on Rue Gay-Lussac for several days. I hope I won't be back too late."

"Well, you know, I'm used to it. Besides, my husband takes my place in the evenings."

Out on the sunny sidewalk, she took her brother's arm.

"It's wonderful, Bob."

Everything was wonderful. The breeze in the air, the shop windows, the passers-by.

"I'm going to show you my little restaurant. And I'm going to have a gin right away. I don't really like brandy, but Albert didn't have anything else in his room."

She had ordered a gin and tonic and her brother had ordered a whisky.

"Did you know this place?"

"No. It seems nice."

"And the food's good, you'll see. It seems funny to me to be talking about food on a day like this, doesn't it?"

"Perhaps it does, a little."

"At lunch I ate twice what I usually eat at home."

They both smiled and gave each other conspiratorial looks.

"It's good to see you, Bob. Do you know what I like about Albert? It's that he's like you in some ways."

"Shall we have dinner? I'm the one who's hungry now."

She saw a word she didn't know on a menu.

"Waiter! 'Porchetta.' What's that?"

"Suckling pig, stuffed and roasted."

"Would you like that, Bob?"

"Yes."

"Two porchettas. Will you have a light chianti with that?"

They were both in a gay mood.

"What time is your train tomorrow?"

"One fifteen."

"I'll go with you to the train."

"I hate saying good-by on station platforms. I'll come by your hotel to say good-by to you."

They stayed for a long time at the table, while at home one only sat down for the precise length of time it took to eat. Once the meal was over there was a kind of stampede to get away.

"Shall we have a coffee with brandy?"

"We'll have something to drink later."

They went along Boulevard Saint-Michel, where the crowded terraces were brightly lit. Odile stared at the spectacle hungrily, as if she had never seen it before. From time to time, when she made a sudden movement, she felt a stab of pain in her wrist, but it did not really hurt.

They did not have a running conversation. It was not really a conversation at all. One of them would say something and the other would echo it. After that they walked in silence for most of the time.

"I've always known you wouldn't stay at home."

"Even when I was a child?"

"From the time you were ten or twelve. You were very precocious."

"Is that bad?"

"No. Don't you think it's a little late for you?"

"You're forgetting what a terrible girl I am."

When they got to the corner of Rue Gay-Lussac they turned around. They were holding hands and Bob was humming.

"You like me, don't you, Bob?"

"Yes."

"Why?"

"I'd find it difficult to say."

"I'm unbearable, am I not?"

"Not if one knows you."

He thought of the medical student. He did not want to hurt his sister, or to discourage her. That was why he added:

"Not even if one doesn't know you at all."

"If I understand you properly, it's the bit in between that's dangerous."

"You're a sweet girl, Odile. You only have one enemy."

"Who?"

"Yourself."

He led her to a terrace where there was a free table.

"We'll have a last drink and then we'll go quietly off to bed."

"Already?"

"What did your student tell you?"

"Yes . . . I'd better rest."

"Well, between ourselves, when do you expect to come to Lausanne?"

"In about a week, if my wrist comes along all right."

"Are you going to spend some time with us?"

"I don't think so. Two days, maybe? Just enough time to pack up my things."

"Shall I still give the guitar away?"

The question embarrassed her a little.

"No. I think I'll take it with me. It's still what I do least badly. And since I only play for myself . . ."

"Mother will be furious."

"I know. But Daddy will understand. He must have known too, a long time ago, that I would go away one day. Did you know Albert has read several of his books?"

"That doesn't surprise me."

They stayed there for a quarter of an hour, relaxed, with no need to talk for the sake of talking.

"What surprises me is the number of people sitting alone . . ."

He did not point out to her that that would be her lot, too, in a week or so.

"Let's go now."

He took her back to her hotel.

"Good night, Bob."

"Good night, Odile."

She watched him striding away. It made her sad to lose him. It was true that in Lausanne she hardly saw him except at mealtimes.

There was no light showing under the door next to

hers. She stopped anyway and listened for a minute, but heard nothing.

She put on her pajamas, then took her make-up off carefully and gently rubbed in a little face cream for the night. Then she took two sleeping pills. After a moment's thought, she took a third.

She fell asleep almost at once, and if she dreamed she did not remember her dreams in the morning.

It was a knocking at the door that woke her up.

"Come in!" she said, thinking it was Bob.

She had not looked at her watch.

"The door is locked."

It was Albert Galabar's voice.

"Have I disturbed you?"

"Just a minute. I'm putting my dressing gown on."

She also ran a comb through her hair.

"I woke you up, didn't I? I forgot to tell you yesterday. It's one of the days when I go on duty at the hospital at eleven o'clock. I don't finish until six. I'd prefer to do your dressing before I go."

His shyness contrasted with his height and his broad shoulders.

"You haven't been in too much pain? Could you sleep?"

"I fell asleep right away."

"At what time?"

"Eleven o'clock. And I've only just waked up."

She lit a cigarette.

"Sit down. Let's see how that wound is getting on."

He removed the dressing of the day before very

carefully. The flesh on either side of the cut had not swollen, and it was hardly red at all.

"It's coming on very well, isn't it?"

"As far as I'm concerned, I can hardly feel it."

"I'm going to put on a new dressing and you'll be all right for twenty-four hours."

"How many stitches did you put in?"

"Five. I thought I'd better play safe. Your skin is very fine, very delicate."

She took that as a compliment and she was pleased.

"Are you going to have a busy day?"

"At the moment I'm on casualty, and one hardly has time to breathe."

"Accidents?"

"Everything."

They were speaking with their lips and the words were only there to hide their thoughts.

She liked him at least as much as she liked Bob, but in a different way.

"Do you go home often?"

"My two sisters are married. They both live in Toulouse. My father and mother are alone at home. I usually try to spend half of each vacation with them in Royan. We rent a big house and my sisters come with their husbands and children."

She was staggered. It was a kind of life that was totally alien to her. She could not see herself at the seaside with parents, married sisters, and their husbands and children.

"Do you expect to settle in Paris?"

"If I can. I'll see you tomorrow, Odile. It'll be Saturday, won't it? In that case, I can come an hour later."

She took her bath as well as she could, trying not to wet the dressing. It was a sort of acrobatics. Then she put on the slacks she had worn the night before.

She opened the window wide. What line were her thoughts taking? The idea of death had left her. And yet she came back to it indirectly. She was waiting for Bob, and he was going to take the train. She imagined the long platforms, and suddenly she found a solution to her problem which had escaped her.

God knows why, a few days before, she had wanted her body not to be identifiable. She believed she had thought of everything, and each time she found an objection that had made the solution impossible.

The train! She had not thought of the train. If she had bought underwear and a dress in a cheap chain store . . . If she had gone to one of the stations in Paris just when an express was arriving . . . She could even have jumped off a railway bridge just before one went by . . .

She felt dizzy, thinking of it. Just to think that she had escaped that made her feel sick and dizzy. For if that idea had occurred to her she would probably have done it.

What had been wrong with her? She no longer understood the decision she had made. She tried in vain to discover how she had arrived at it.

She rang for the boy to bring up her breakfast.

"May I have two fried eggs?"

She was hungry. Usually she just had toast and marmalade.

"And a big glass of orange juice, please."

She did not know what to do or where to go. Usually she was still asleep at that time, and here she was all ready.

But ready for what? She had nothing to do.

Bob arrived while she was eating by the window.

"I see you're not lacking in appetite."

"No. Do you know, Albert has been in already to put a new dressing on. He's on duty at eleven o'clock."

"Did you sleep well? You didn't feel any pain?"

"I slept as I have rarely done, and when I woke up I had forgotten I had a cut on my wrist. Would you like something to eat? Aren't you going to have any lunch?"

"I'll have lunch on the train."

She lit a cigarette, and he took one too.

"I want to ask you to do something. It's not to wait a week before you come home. Our parents are going to be very upset, particularly when they know your decision. They mustn't think that you're leaving home because of them."

"I'll promise you that, Bob."

"When they see you looking so well, they'll think that for one reason or another you pretended to commit suicide."

"Did you ever think that?"

"No. But I haven't got a suspicious character. Mother is naturally suspicious."

"I know. Do you like this room?"

"It's more cheerful than the one I had at Monsieur Bedon's. It must be more expensive, too."

"I haven't asked the price."

"That's just like you."

"I'll try to stay here."

"Have you any plans?"

"Not any real plans. I must take my ignorance into account. I must find a job that's easy and at the same time not too unpleasant. I wouldn't be able, for example, to work in a factory. I couldn't be a shampooist at a hairdresser's, either.

"If I could choose anything I wanted, I'd be a nurse. In Lausanne, I found out about the courses. I don't have enough basic training to make good at it."

"Poor Odile! You've barely caught your breath and here I am asking you such a question today."

"That's all right. Don't think I'm not thinking about it, even when I don't talk about it. There are two things I could do. I could be a receptionist in an office —that doesn't need special skills—or a switchboard operator. But switchboard girls are almost always shut up all day in a little room, and the time must drag for them."

"Do you know, you've got a good idea."

She shrugged her shoulders.

"I've always had plenty of ideas, dear Bob, but at the last moment they would fade into nothing. I can see myself very well in a doctor's outer office, or a dentist's, or a lawyer's. I'd prefer a doctor's or a dentist's."

"I hope that's what you'll tell us when you get back home."

"I'm going to start going through the advertisements in the papers. If there's nothing there, I'll put one in."

"I've got to go now."

"Haven't you any luggage?"

"I left my suitcase downstairs."

"I suppose you'll get a taxi on Boulevard Saint-Michel."

"Yes."

"I'll go with you. Don't worry, I won't go any further."

She put her jacket on and picked up her handbag.

She remembered to lock the door as she went out, and gave the key to the proprietress. The baby was not on the floor.

"Is he having a nap already?" she asked.

"He has his bottle at noon and goes to sleep right after."

Bob almost forgot his suitcase.

"And I'm the one who has always accused you of being scatterbrained!"

They had only two hundred yards to walk. There was a whole row of taxis. Most people were having lunch. One could see some of them, too, in the bars, having a drink just before lunch.

"Good-by, Bob. And thank you again. You don't know how happy you've made me by coming . . ."

"That's all right. Be good now. Get a grip on yourself and come and see us in good shape."

He gave her a kiss, put his hands on her shoulders, and looked her straight in the eyes.

"Don't be afraid: you'll never be all alone."

He got into the taxi, and she could not ask him what he meant. Was he talking about himself? It was unlikely and out of character. Did he mean the medical student? Was he trying to make her understand that there would always be a man in her life?

She walked as far as Boulevard Saint-Germain and turned to the right. There were a lot of free tables on the terrace at Deux Magots, and she sat down and ordered a gin and tonic.

She must get out of the habit of drinking. Before, she drank only fruit juice. It was in the night places in Lausanne that she had got into the habit of drinking liquor.

She had chosen the one she found had the least taste: gin.

But it was the same with drinking as with smoking. It became a habit. She used to have a bottle in her room, she who had been annoyed with her mother for drinking two or three whiskies while playing bridge.

Now she was on vacation, between two periods of

164

her life. She had to keep her mind free and let herself live. That would require no effort on her part. The late autumn was magnificent and the sun was dancing about in the leaves of the trees. Most women were still wearing their summer clothes.

She half shut her eyes. Blurred figures passed by in front of the terrace, and she told herself it was good to be alive.

_____

Chapter 7

Albert came to see her every day, to take off the old dressing and put on a new one. The wound remained clean, without the slightest inflammation.

Contrary to Odile's expectations, he became more distant as time went on. Preoccupied, he hardly spoke to her, or if he did it was to ask tiresome questions.

"If I understand you rightly, you've always lived in the same house. Is that so?"

"So has my father. And my grandfather, who had a beautiful white beard and who died when I was nine."

She bought several newspapers and read the advertisements carefully. They asked for typists, stenographers with a perfect knowledge of English, specialists of all kinds.

Once someone wanted a switchboard operator, but she had to speak German as well as English and French.

She did not grow discouraged.

"Do you still take the tranquilizers your doctor in Lausanne prescribed?"

"Yes."

"You don't need them any more. You could do without them very well. The best thing would be to talk to him about it when you go home."

Once he asked her a more personal question.

"Why did you leave school?"

"Because I was bored. It seemed to me that what they were teaching me was useless. I had begun to go out in the evenings. In the mornings I felt sleepy. All the girls were against me . . ."

Seen in perspective, that had lost its importance, and she laughed at herself for having made a song and dance about it.

She went to the movies almost every day, and tried out new restaurants.

"Arriving saturday's t.e.e."

She had sent that telegram to Bob and she was surprised to see her father on the station platform. As she moved along with the queue of travelers, she looked at him and found that he was different. It was impossible that he had changed in two weeks. It was she who was seeing him differently.

He had always been plump; now she saw him as fat and flabby. Even the station seemed less big and had something of a backwater about it.

"Have you any bags, Mademoiselle Pointet?"

"I have only this little suitcase."

Her father watched her approaching and seemed

moved. He kissed her on both cheeks, awkwardly, because at home they kissed each other very little.

"Your brother has been very kind. He let me take his place."

He was pretending to take this meeting very lightly.

"Give me something to carry."

To make him happy she gave him her toilet case.

"Have you had a good trip?"

"It's so short, you know . . ."

"You haven't got any thinner."

"No. I'm eating very well."

"Your mother has been very worried."

They walked through the underpass, coming up not far from the taxi rank.

"Avenue de Jaman. The first house on the right."

"I know where it is, Monsieur Pointet."

Everything had changed, the place and the people. She did not feel at home any more. She felt like a traveler in a strange city.

She had lived here for more than eighteen years. Her father and mother had spent all their lives there.

Her mother ran out as soon as they opened the garden gate.

"My poor little girl," she said, kissing her.

She was sniffling. She was crying. She was looking at her as though at a ghost.

"Have you been in much pain?"

"I haven't had any pain at all."

"Come inside quickly. It's colder here than it is in Paris. You're thinner, aren't you?"

"No. I think I have even put on some weight."

The three of them went into the house.

"Your brother has a class. He'll be back soon."

She did not know what to say to them. She felt with them the way she did with strangers. The drawing room seemed more dismal than her room in the Hôtel Héliard, opposite the Gare de Lyon. And yet her grandfather had worked in there for more than forty years and it was there that her mother played bridge with her friends.

She had promised herself she would stay for two days. Now she was wondering how she could manage to cut her stay short.

"Have you any gin?" she asked her father.

He was surprised and nodded.

"Could I have one? The train ride has upset me a bit."

It was not true, but she needed something before she faced the house.

Mathilde came in her turn to give her a kiss.

"But you look very well!"

She was sniffling too, and wiping her eyes with a corner of her apron.

"I hope you won't be going away again this time. There's nowhere better than home."

They were all three looking at her, and she decided to get to the point straight away.

"I'm going away again in two days."

"Going where?" her mother asked suspiciously.

"To Paris, of course."

"And you've made this decision alone, without discussing it with us?"

"I have the right to make a decision on which my whole future depends."

"And what are you going to do there?"

Her voice was getting aggressive.

"I shall work."

"What at? You haven't any training."

"I'm going to be a doctor's receptionist."

"Have you found a job already?"

She lied.

"Yes. And I've taken a little room at the hotel."

Her father gave her a drink and had one himself at the same time.

"Your health."

She knew he would back her up.

"So, you're going to leave us and live alone in Paris."

"I couldn't live here any more. I've tried. You know what happened."

"Don't you think that after a few weeks you'll have had enough?"

"If I've had enough I'll come home."

"Well! If I could only believe that! How's your arm?"

"My arm is getting on very well. The wound will soon be closed and I won't even need a dressing."

"Aren't you hungry?"

"No. I ate on the train."

It was almost seven o'clock. The lights were lit. They had to be lighted early, because the house was dark.

"Won't you eat with us anyway?"

"If you want me to."

They could hear Bob's motorbike. He put it in the garage and came into the house.

He hugged his sister, crying:

"Not too upset to be back in our old house?"

He winked at her.

"No, not too upset."

He looked at his parents and, seeing his mother's pinched face, understood what had happened.

"When are you going back?"

"In two days."

"How did you know she wasn't going to stay here?" his mother asked.

"Because I know Odile and I saw her in Paris."

"Do you know what she wants to do?"

"No."

"She wants to be a doctor's receptionist."

"That's not a bad idea."

"Do you think she's right?"

"She's old enough to decide. After all, it's her life."

Mathilde came in to tell them that dinner was served. Before leaving the drawing room, Odile drank a glass of gin at one swallow.

"Did you start to drink in Paris?"

"No. It was here. Everyone in the house drinks except Bob, who does it only exceptionally."

"Not everyone is eighteen."

Dinner was torture for her. She had a sensation of stifling. Except for her brother, they looked at her again and again as if she had suddenly become a freak.

Her mother was the most bitter and the most incredulous.

"Whom are you going with in Paris?"

"With no one."

"Isn't there someone you're going back to be with?"

She almost blushed, thinking of Albert. Bob gave her a stealthy glance.

"I'm not going back to be with anybody."

"Do you think it will be fun living by yourself every day?"

"I've just had some experience of that and I haven't been bored for a minute."

"While you do get bored here?"

"I didn't say that."

"But you were thinking it."

"I like to live by myself."

She hardly knew what she was eating, and she thought of her good appetite in Paris.

When the meal was over she said good night.

"I'm going up to my room. I need to organize my things."

Bob carried her suitcase up for her, went into her room, and sat down on the edge of her bed.

"You really take the bull by the horns, don't you?"

"I had to. Tomorrow it would be worse."

"Maybe you're right."

"I'm sorry for Daddy—I've hurt him. He seemed older to me, less sure of himself."

"You're forgetting he's already had his two bottles."

"I know, but I didn't see him like that. It's not the first time I've been away for a few days. This time I feel everything has changed."

"Even me?"

"Idiot!"

"You know, I'm very likely to lead a life like theirs sometime. Not in this house, which has had its day. But a well-regulated life, centered about my work."

"And about your wife."

"If I get married. At the moment I don't have any desire to. How's your young doctor?"

"He isn't a doctor yet."

"All right. Your young student."

"He's been in every day to put a new dressing on."

"Are you in love with him?"

"I don't know."

"What about him?"

"He gets shyer and shyer."

"Because he's scared to say anything."

"I thought that for a while, but I'm not so sure any more."

"Have you kept your room?"

"Yes."

"Is it true, this story about you being a reception-ist?"

"No. But I hope it will be. I'll put an advertisement in the papers when I get back."

She opened her wardrobe and threw in a pile on the floor all the clothes she had not thought she would wear any more.

"When I think I was keeping all these old things . . ."

"You can't wear jeans when you're a receptionist."

"I'll wear a dress."

He watched her in amazement as she moved around. The house had not changed. Nor had their parents. It was she who had changed.

"Are you going to see Doctor Vinet?"

"Why should I? I'm not ill."

It was the first time she had ever said that. Before, she had always been worried about her health and complained about the most unlikely illnesses.

"He'll be sad if he learns you've been here without seeing him."

"I'll see tomorrow. I might call him up."

"It's Sunday."

"He has been to see me on a Sunday before, or else I've been to his office."

He looked at the pile of clothes and underwear that she was getting rid of.

"You won't have anything left to wear, will you?"

"If it were possible I would throw out everything,

everything that reminds me of the past, and I would only wear new things."

She laughed.

"You see, I'm still extravagant."

"I'm going to miss you."

"I'll miss you too. You're my only friend. I hope you'll come to see me from time to time."

Albert Pointet kept the same schedule on Sundays as on other days. After his walk he would go up to his attic, carrying his two bottles, and he would sit down at the table he used for a desk.

He heard light footsteps on the stairs at about nine o'clock. He did not think it could be his daughter at that hour, and yet it was.

"Am I disturbing you?"

"No. Sit down. Have you had your breakfast?"

"I've just had it."

"Is your mother up?"

"If she is, she hasn't come down yet."

"Don't be angry with her. It has given me a shock, too. We're used to there being four of us here, to seeing each other twice a day at table."

"Where nobody says anything."

"Because everyone has different interests. Have you ever thought that for parents of children who have grown up, it's possibly out of a sense of modesty? We don't want to bore you with stories of what we are doing, and we don't dare to ask you what you do."

He looked at her with a melancholy expression. "How are you going to get along, as to money?"

"I shall be working."

"I know, but you won't be earning enough to live in the way you are used to. I thought about it in bed last night. We provide for Bob until he finishes his studies, and I give him pocket money as well."

"That's natural, isn't it? If one didn't do that there wouldn't be any students."

"Let's suppose that you were in the same situation, that you had been continuing your studies, here or in Paris. I would provide for your needs until you earned enough to live on."

"I hadn't thought about that."

"What you're going to do is a sort of training. So I'll do as I would if you were a student, and I'll give you an allowance until you're twenty-five."

She stayed still for a moment, staring incredulously at her father.

"Will you really do that?"

"Yes."

Then she rushed to him and kissed him very hard on his bearded cheeks.

"You're lovely, Daddy."

"You don't need to tell your mother about it. Not yet. I'll know when it's the right moment to tell her the truth."

"You do undertand, don't you, that I'm not running away from you?"

"I understand. When you were a little girl you often used to come up to see me. You would sit in a corner and watch me writing. Is it tomorrow you're going away?"

"Tomorrow evening, on the T.E.E. again."

"This time I won't be at the station. I don't want to show everyone my feelings."

Chapter **8**

She had gone back to her room on Rue de la Harpe. She had had dinner on the train. It was after eleven at night, but she needed to go out and feel herself rubbing elbows with the crowd. There had been no light under Albert Galabar's door, and she had been disappointed at that. Was she jealous already? Perhaps.

Wasn't it normal that at his age he should have one woman or more in his life?

She found a bar with high stools near Saint-Germain-des-Prés. She asked for a gin.

She looked around her greedily, and she wanted to listen to music. There was some not far from there. She felt a bit uncomfortable among a very chic, very dressy clientele.

Her father had been marvelous. A little before she left, he had gone up to her room to give her a bank note, a thousand Swiss francs.

"I'll send you the same amount every month, by bank draft. You'll need extra money at first."

"I asked Bob to send my motorbike. Is that all right?"

"Of course. It's yours."

"I'm taking my guitar too. It's the only thing I do reasonably well."

She liked to sit on the edge of her bed and run her fingers over the strings.

"I've taken my record player too . . . I hope you're not angry with me."

"No. I understand."

He had not wept. He had taken her as far as the taxi, with Bob. Her mother had stayed in the drawing room, where she had pulled aside the curtain.

"I only ask you to be careful."

"I promise you that. I'd rather no one came to the station."

Her luggage was cumbersome, and she had to get a porter.

"Are you going to live in Paris?" the man asked, surprised.

He knew her well. He had often carried her bags.

"Well, I've grown up now, haven't I?"

She went back to the hotel and decided to unpack her bags. She put the guitar in a corner of the room, the record player on one of the two bedside tables. She put a record on while she hung her clothes in the wardrobe and in the cupboard. There was just enough room. It was the same with the drawers, which would not have held more than her underwear.

She took her sleeping pills. She had not seen Doctor Vinet. She had tried to call him on Sunday morning, but he must have been away for the weekend with his wife.

She could not reach him the next morning either, for he was on duty at the Nestlé Hospital.

She put her empty suitcases in the corridor. She felt she was at home at last, and it didn't take her long to go to sleep.

She got up a little before nine o'clock and had her breakfast sent up. Then she took a bath and dressed. Her movements were a bit slow, and she felt a little like a convalescent. She must work herself slowly into her new life.

The student must have heard her moving around, for he knocked on her door at ten o'clock.

He looked at her with some curiosity.

"I didn't know you were coming back so soon."

"I couldn't have stayed any longer. I felt a stranger there, and I hated myself for it."

"Did you see your doctor?"

"No. He wasn't at home on Sunday and he's on duty at the hospital on Monday mornings."

"Have you had any pain?"

"None at all."

Each sat down in the usual place, and the young man took the dressing off.

"That's marvelous. It has already begun to heal. I

think I'll just cover it with a gauze pad and some adhesive tape."

"I have some good news for you."

"What?"

"I have a job starting next month."

"You've found a job? In Paris?"

"And with a doctor. Thanks to my dressing, in fact. I went to have dinner in the dining car. I was put at a table for two. Opposite me there was a middle-aged man. He seemed quite pleasant.

"Toward the middle of the meal he asked me if I had been severely hurt.

" 'Do forgive me for speaking to you when we haven't been introduced. I am Doctor Le Flem.' "

"The cardiologist?"

"I don't know. He didn't tell me what he was a specialist in. He lives in Place Denfert-Rochereau. I felt at ease with him. I was sure that he wouldn't try anything wrong with me. I told him I only had a cut on my wrist and it was almost healed.

"He didn't ask me how I had hurt myself but only if I lived in Paris, and I told him I was in the process of moving there.

" 'Are you a student?'

" 'No. I've never got my school-learning certificate.'

" 'What are you going to do?'

" 'I'd like to find a job as a receptionist, preferably with a doctor or a dentist.'

"He began to think, then he took a visiting card out of his wallet.

"'Listen. Here is my address. I'm always in my office in the afternoon. Come and see me. I may be able to give you a job. My receptionist, who got married last year, is expecting a baby around Christmas. I must have a word with her and ask her what she is going to do. Where do you live?'

"'Until now I have lived in Lausanne with my parents. I've just told them that I'm going to live in Paris. Here I'm in a hotel on Rue de la Harpe.'

"'It's not far away.'

"'I have a motorbike.'"

Albert was looking at her closely.

"Will you stay in this hotel rather than take a room nearer your work?"

"I'm going to stay here."

He did not ask why.

"Would you feel better with a lighter bandage?"

"Yes. Thank you, Doctor."

"May I shake your hand to congratulate you?"

He seemed strangely moved.

"I'll leave you now. You must have to straighten out your things."

"I did almost all of that last night."

"You're going to be working during the day."

"I'll get used to it. You can see I'm already dressed and have had breakfast."

She took her guitar from the corner and, alone in

her room, began to play some chords. Suddenly she felt a bit frightened. Things were going too well. She knew her own character, and since her trip to Lausanne she knew she would never go back to her former life.

She had not heard her neighbor go out. She took something out of her brief case, her father's revolver, which she had forgotten to mention to him.

The next moment, she was knocking on the door next to hers. He was sitting at his table, which had notebooks spread all over it.

He watched her come toward him, the gun in her hand. For a moment he looked startled.

"Would you look after this for me?"

"Of course. Are you still afraid you might?"

"I don't think so. It's more a symbol, you know."

He began a sentence that he did not finish.

"Why . . ."

He was going to say:

"Why me?"

Then he looked at her.

She said, quickly:

"I'll let you get back to work."

"Yes."

Later, perhaps.

He watched her as she went toward the door.

Epalinges, October 4, 1970